Ruskin Bond has been writing for over sixty years, and now has over 120 titles in print—novels, collections of short stories, poetry, essays, anthologies and books for children. His first novel, *The Room on the Roof*, received the prestigious John Llewellyn Rhys Prize in 1957. He has also received the Padma Shri (1999), the Padma Bhushan (2014) and two awards from Sahitya Akademi—one for his short stories and another for his writings for children. In 2012, the Delhi Government gave him its Lifetime Achievement Award.

Born in 1934, Ruskin Bond grew up in Jamnagar, Shimla, New Delhi and Dehradun. Apart from three years in the UK, he has spent all his life in India, and now lives in Mussoorie with his adopted family.

Published by
Rupa Publications India Pvt. Ltd 2020
7/16, Ansari Road, Daryaganj
New Delhi 110002

Sales centres:
Prayagraj Bengaluru Chennai
Hyderabad Jaipur Kathmandu
Kolkata Mumbai

ISBN: 978-93-89967-22-7

Second impression 2023

10 9 8 7 6 5 4 3 2

Printed in India

Stories from My Childhood

Selected and Compiled by

RUSKIN BOND

RUPA

Contents

Introduction

We don't become writers for life unless we have been avid readers in our childhood and youth. Writing books is not a simple task, and it takes a lover of books to write a book.

The first six years of my life were spent in Jamnagar, then a small post on the west coast of India. It was a princely state, and my father had started a small school for the palace children. But there were no bookshops in Jamnagar, not even a railway station bookstall. I possessed two books—a big book of nursery rhymes, and a battered and well-read copy of *Alice in Wonderland.*

With the help of my father I read *Alice* several times, and it did not take me long to know all the nursery rhymes by heart. I can still recite most of them.

It was only when I was a little older and was sent to a boarding school in Shimla that I became a true reader—someone who couldn't do without books. I must have been eleven when I read Dickens' *David Copperfield* and Hugh Walpole's *Fortitude* and these two books sowed the seeds of my ambition to become a writer. And I still recall the opening lines of *Fortitude*: 'It isn't life that matters, but the courage you bring to it.'

As a senior boy I was put in charge of the school library, and given the keys to it. This meant that I could go to the library whenever I wanted, and I made full use of this privilege. In the remaining four years at my school, I must have read well over a hundred books, the authors including Dickens, George Eliot, Conrad, J.M. Barrie, Stevenson, Somerset Maugham, J.B. Priestley, Graham Greene, Tagore, Maupassant,

Emile Zola, P.G. Wodehouse and Agatha Christie! A motley crew, you might say. No wonder I flunked my mathematics paper.

But I was going to be a writer, not an accountant.

All that early reading gave me a terrific foundation for the literary life. I may sometimes take a day or two off from writing, but I have never taken time off from reading. There is always a book at my bedside or on my desk or beside an easychair.

Sometimes I think I am a reader first and a writer second. And why not? Life is often like the Mad Tea Party in *Alice*, and it takes great writing to bring some sanity back to it.

Ruskin Bond

February, 2020

A Mad Tea-Party

LEWIS CAROLL

There was a table set out under a tree in front of the house, and the March Hare and the Hatter were having tea at it: a Dormouse was sitting between them, fast asleep, and the other two were using it as a cushion, resting their elbows on it, and talking over its head. 'Very uncomfortable for the Dormouse,' thought Alice; 'only, as it's asleep, I suppose it doesn't mind.'

The table was a large one, but the three were all crowded together at one corner of it: 'No room! No room!' they cried out when they saw Alice coming. 'There's PLENTY of room!' said Alice indignantly, and she sat down in a large arm-chair at one end of the table.

'Have some wine,' the March Hare said in an encouraging tone.

Alice looked all round the table, but there was nothing on it but tea. 'I don't see any wine,' she remarked.

'There isn't any,' said the March Hare.

'Then it wasn't very civil of you to offer it,' said Alice angrily.

'It wasn't very civil of you to sit down without being invited,' said the March Hare.

'I didn't know it was YOUR table,' said Alice; 'it's laid for a great many more than three.'

'Your hair wants cutting,' said the Hatter. He had been

looking at Alice for some time with great curiosity, and this was his first speech.

'You should learn not to make personal remarks,' Alice said with some severity; 'it's very rude.'

The Hatter opened his eyes very wide on hearing this; but all he SAID was, 'Why is a raven like a writing-desk?'

'Come, we shall have some fun now!' thought Alice. 'I'm glad they've begun asking riddles.—I believe I can guess that,' she added aloud.

'Do you mean that you think you can find out the answer to it?' said the March Hare.

'Exactly so,' said Alice.

'Then you should say what you mean,' the March Hare went on.

'I do,' Alice hastily replied; 'at least—at least I mean what I say—that's the same thing, you know.'

'Not the same thing a bit!' said the Hatter. 'You might just as well say that 'I see what I eat' is the same thing as 'I eat what I see'!'

'You might just as well say,' added the March Hare, 'that 'I like what I get' is the same thing as 'I get what I like'!'

'You might just as well say,' added the Dormouse, who seemed to be talking in his sleep, 'that 'I breathe when I sleep' is the same thing as 'I sleep when I breathe'!'

'It IS the same thing with you,' said the Hatter, and here the conversation dropped, and the party sat silent for a minute, while Alice thought over all she could remember about ravens and writing-desks, which wasn't much.

The Hatter was the first to break the silence. 'What day of the month is it?' he said, turning to Alice: he had taken his watch out of his pocket, and was looking at it uneasily, shaking it every now and then, and holding it to his ear.

Alice considered a little, and then said 'The fourth.'

'Two days wrong!' sighed the Hatter. 'I told you butter wouldn't suit the works!' he added looking angrily at the March Hare.

'It was the BEST butter,' the March Hare meekly replied.

'Yes, but some crumbs must have got in as well,' the Hatter grumbled: 'you shouldn't have put it in with the bread-knife.'

The March Hare took the watch and looked at it gloomily: then he dipped it into his cup of tea, and looked at it again: but he could think of nothing better to say than his first remark, 'It was the BEST butter, you know.'

Alice had been looking over his shoulder with some curiosity. 'What a funny watch!' she remarked. 'It tells the day of the month, and doesn't tell what o'clock it is!'

'Why should it?' muttered the Hatter. 'Does YOUR watch tell you what year it is?'

'Of course not,' Alice replied very readily: 'but that's because it stays the same year for such a long time together.'

'Which is just the case with MINE,' said the Hatter.

Alice felt dreadfully puzzled. The Hatter's remark seemed to have no sort of meaning in it, and yet it was certainly English. 'I don't quite understand you,' she said, as politely as she could.

'The Dormouse is asleep again,' said the Hatter, and he poured a little hot tea upon its nose.

The Dormouse shook its head impatiently, and said, without opening its eyes, 'Of course, of course; just what I was going to remark myself.'

'Have you guessed the riddle yet?' the Hatter said, turning to Alice again.

'No, I give it up,' Alice replied: 'what's the answer?'

'I haven't the slightest idea,' said the Hatter.

'Nor I,' said the March Hare.

Alice sighed wearily. 'I think you might do something better with the time,' she said, 'than waste it in asking riddles that have no answers.'

'If you knew Time as well as I do,' said the Hatter, 'you wouldn't talk about wasting IT. It's HIM.'

'I don't know what you mean,' said Alice.

'Of course you don't!' the Hatter said, tossing his head contemptuously. 'I dare say you never even spoke to Time!'

'Perhaps not,' Alice cautiously replied: 'but I know I have to beat time when I learn music.'

'Ah! that accounts for it,' said the Hatter. 'He won't stand beating. Now, if you only kept on good terms with him, he'd do almost anything you liked with the clock. For instance, suppose it were nine o'clock in the morning, just time to begin lessons: you'd only have to whisper a hint to Time, and round goes the clock in a twinkling! Half-past one, time for dinner!'

('I only wish it was,' the March Hare said to itself in a whisper.)

'That would be grand, certainly,' said Alice thoughtfully: 'but then—I shouldn't be hungry for it, you know.'

'Not at first, perhaps,' said the Hatter: 'but you could keep it to half-past one as long as you liked.'

'Is that the way YOU manage?' Alice asked.

The Hatter shook his head mournfully. 'Not I!' he replied. 'We quarrelled last March—just before HE went mad, you know—'(pointing with his tea spoon at the March Hare,) '—it was at the great concert given by the Queen of Hearts, and I had to sing

'Twinkle, twinkle, little bat!
How I wonder what you're at!'

You know the song, perhaps?'

'I've heard something like it,' said Alice. 'It goes on, you know,' the Hatter continued, 'in this way:

'Up above the world you fly,
Like a tea-tray in the sky.
Twinkle, twinkle—'

Here the Dormouse shook itself, and began singing in its sleep 'Twinkle, twinkle, twinkle, twinkle—' and went on so long that they had to pinch it to make it stop.

'Well, I'd hardly finished the first verse,' said the Hatter, 'when the Queen jumped up and bawled out, 'He's murdering the time! Off with his head!'

'How dreadfully savage!' exclaimed Alice.

'And ever since that,' the Hatter went on in a mournful tone, 'he won't do a thing I ask! It's always six o'clock now.'

A bright idea came into Alice's head. 'Is that the reason so many tea-things are put out here?' she asked.

'Yes, that's it,' said the Hatter with a sigh: 'it's always tea-time, and we've no time to wash the things between whiles.'

'Then you keep moving round, I suppose?' said Alice.

'Exactly so,' said the Hatter: 'as the things get used up.'

'But what happens when you come to the beginning again?' Alice ventured to ask.

'Suppose we change the subject,' the March Hare interrupted, yawning. 'I'm getting tired of this. I vote the young lady tells us a story.'

'I'm afraid I don't know one,' said Alice, rather alarmed at the proposal.

'Then the Dormouse shall!' they both cried. 'Wake up, Dormouse!' And they pinched it on both sides at once.

The Dormouse slowly opened his eyes. 'I wasn't asleep,' he said in a hoarse, feeble voice: 'I heard every word you fellows were saying.'

'Tell us a story!' said the March Hare.

'Yes, please do!' pleaded Alice.

'And be quick about it,' added the Hatter, 'or you'll be asleep again before it's done.'

'Once upon a time there were three little sisters,' the Dormouse began in a great hurry; 'and their names were Elsie, Lacie, and Tillie; and they lived at the bottom of a well—'

'What did they live on?' said Alice, who always took a great interest in questions of eating and drinking.

'They lived on treacle,' said the Dormouse, after thinking a minute or two.

'They couldn't have done that, you know,' Alice gently remarked; 'they'd have been ill.'

'So they were,' said the Dormouse, 'VERY ill.'

Alice tried to fancy to herself what such an extraordinary ways of living would be like, but it puzzled her too much, so she went on: 'But why did they live at the bottom of a well?'

'Take some more tea,' the March Hare said to Alice, very earnestly.

'I've had nothing yet,' Alice replied in an offended tone, 'so I can't take more.'

'You mean you can't take LESS,' said the Hatter: 'it's very easy to take MORE than nothing.'

'Nobody asked YOUR opinion,' said Alice.

'Who's making personal remarks now?' the Hatter asked triumphantly.

Alice did not quite know what to say to this; so she helped herself to some tea and bread-and-butter, and then turned to the Dormouse, and repeated her question. 'Why did they live at the bottom of a well?'

The Dormouse again took a minute or two to think about it, and then said, 'It was a treacle-well.'

'There's no such thing!' Alice was beginning very angrily, but the Hatter and the March Hare went 'Sh! sh!' and the Dormouse sulkily remarked, 'If you can't be civil, you'd better finish the story for yourself.'

'No, please go on!' Alice said very humbly; 'I won't interrupt again. I dare say there may be ONE.'

'One, indeed!' said the Dormouse indignantly. However, he consented to go on. 'And so these three little sisters—they were learning to draw, you know—'

'What did they draw?' said Alice, quite forgetting her promise.

'Treacle,' said the Dormouse, without considering at all this time.

'I want a clean cup,' interrupted the Hatter: 'let's all move one place on.'

He moved on as he spoke, and the Dormouse followed him: the March Hare moved into the Dormouse's place, and Alice rather unwillingly took the place of the March Hare. The Hatter was the only one who got any advantage from the change: and Alice was a good deal worse off than before, as the March Hare had just upset the milk-jug into his plate.

Alice did not wish to offend the Dormouse again, so she began very cautiously: 'But I don't understand. Where did they draw the treacle from?'

'You can draw water out of a water-well,' said the Hatter; 'so I should think you could draw treacle out of a treacle-well—eh, stupid?'

'But they were IN the well,' Alice said to the Dormouse, not choosing to notice this last remark.

'Of course they were', said the Dormouse; '—well in.'

This answer so confused poor Alice, that she let the Dormouse go on for some time without interrupting it. 'They were learning to draw,' the Dormouse went on, yawning and rubbing its eyes, for it was getting very sleepy; 'and they drew all manner of things—everything that begins with an M—'

'Why with an M?' said Alice.

'Why not?' said the March Hare.

Alice was silent.

The Dormouse had closed its eyes by this time, and was going off into a doze; but, on being pinched by the Hatter, it woke up again with a little shriek, and went on: '—that begins with an M, such as mouse-traps, and the moon, and memory, and muchness—you know you say things are "much of a muchness"—did you ever see such a thing as a drawing of a muchness?'

'Really, now you ask me,' said Alice, very much confused, 'I don't think—'

'Then you shouldn't talk,' said the Hatter.

This piece of rudeness was more than Alice could bear: she got up in great disgust, and walked off; the Dormouse fell asleep instantly, and neither of the others took the least notice of her going, though she looked back once or twice, half hoping that they would call after her: the last time she saw them, they were trying to put the Dormouse into the teapot.

'At any rate I'll never go THERE again!' said Alice as she picked her way through the wood. 'It's the stupidest tea-party I ever was at in all my life!'

Just as she said this, she noticed that one of the trees had a door leading right into it. 'That's very curious!' she thought. 'But everything's curious today. I think I may as well go in at once.' And in she went.

Once more she found herself in the long hall, and close to the little glass table. 'Now, I'll manage better this time,' she said to herself, and began by taking the little golden key, and unlocking the door that led into the garden. Then she went to work nibbling at the mushroom (she had kept a piece of it in her pocket) till she was about a foot high: then she walked down the little passage: and THEN—she found herself at last in the beautiful garden, among the bright flower-beds and the cool fountains.

The Diverting History of John Gilpin

WILLIAM COWPER

John Gilpin was a citizen
  Of credit and renown,
A train-band captain eke was he,
  Of famous London town.

John Gilpin's spouse said to her dear,
  'Though wedded we have been
These twice ten tedious years, yet we
  No holiday have seen.

'To-morrow is our wedding-day,
  And we will then repair
Unto the 'Bell' at Edmonton,
  All in a chaise and pair.

'My sister, and my sister's child,
  Myself, and children three,
Will fill the chaise; so you must ride
  On horseback after we.'

He soon replied, 'I do admire
  Of womankind but one,

And you are she, my dearest dear,
  Therefore it shall be done.

'I am a linendraper bold,
  As all the world doth know,
And my good friend the calender
  Will lend his horse to go.'

Quoth Mrs Gilpin, 'That's well said;
  And for that wine is dear,
We will be furnished with our own,
  Which is both bright and clear.'

John Gilpin kissed his loving wife.
  O'erjoyed was he to find.
That though on pleasure she was bent,
  She had a frugal mind.

The morning came, the chaise was brought,
  But yet was not allowed
To drive up to the door, lest all
  Should say that she was proud.

So three doors off the chaise was stayed,
  Where they did all get in;
Six precious souls, and all agog
  To dash through thick and thin.

Smack went the whip, round went the wheels,
  Were never folks so glad!
The stones did rattle underneath,
  As if Cheapside were mad.

John Gilpin at his horse's side
  Seized fast the flowing mane,

And up he got, in haste to ride,
  But soon came down again.

For saddletree scarce reached had he,
  His journey to begin,
When, turning round his head, he saw
  Three customers come in.

So down he came; for loss of time,
  Although it grieved him sore,
Yet loss of pence, full well he knew,
  Would trouble him much more.

'Twas long before the customers
  Were suited to their mind,
When Betty screaming came downstairs,
  'The wine is left behind!'

'Good lack!' quoth he, 'yet bring it me,
  My leathern belt likewise,
In which I bear my trusty sword
  When I do exercise.'

Now Mistress Gilpin (careful soul!)
  Had two stone bottles found,
To hold the liquor that she loved,
  And keep it safe and sound.

Each bottle had a curling ear,
  Through which the belt he drew,
And hung a bottle on each side,
  To make his balance true.

Then over all, that he might be
  Equipped from top to toe,

His long red cloak, well brushed and neat,
He manfully did throw.

Now see him mounted once again
Upon his nimble steed,
Full slowly pacing o'er the stones,
With caution and good heed.

But finding soon a smoother road
Beneath his well-shod feet,
The snorting beast began to trot,
Which galled him in his seat.

'So, fair and softly!' John he cried,
But John he cried in vain;
That trot became a gallop soon,
In spite of curb and rein.

So stooping down, as needs he must
Who cannot sit upright,
He grasped the mane with both his hands,
And eke with all his might.

His horse, who never in that sort
Had handled been before,
What thing upon his back had got,
Did wonder more and more.

Away went Gilpin, neck or nought,
Away went hat and wig;
He little dreamt, when he set out,
Of running such a rig.

The wind did blow, the cloak did fly
Like streamer long and gay,

Till, loop and button failing both,
  At last it flew away.

Then might all people well discern
  The bottles he had slung;
A bottle swinging at each side,
  As hath been said or sung.

The dogs did bark, the children screamed,
  Up flew the windows all;
And every soul cried out, 'Well done!'
  As loud as he could bawl.

Away went Gilpin—who but he?
  His fame soon spread around;
'He carries weight! he rides a race!
  'Tis for a thousand pound!'

And still as fast as he drew near,
  'Twas wonderful to view
How in a trice the turnpike-men
  Their gates wide open threw.

And now, as he went bowing down
  His reeking head full low,
The bottles twain behind his back
  Were shattered at a blow.

Down ran the wine into the road,
  Most piteous to be seen,
Which made the horse's flanks to smoke,
  As they had basted been.

But still he seemed to carry weight.
  With leathern girdle braced;

For all might see the bottle-necks
  Still dangling at his waist.

Thus all through merry Islington
  These gambols he did play,
Until he came unto the Wash
  Of Edmonton so gay;

And there he threw the wash about
  On both sides of the way,
Just like unto a trundling mop,
  Or a wild goose at play.

At Edmonton his loving wife
  From the balcony spied
Her tender husband, wondering much
  To see how he did ride.

'Stop, stop, John Gilpin!—Here's the house!'
  They all at once did cry;
'The dinner waits, and we are tired';
  Said Gilpin—'So am I!'

But yet his horse was not a whit
  Inclined to tarry there;
For why?—his owner had a house
  Full ten miles off, at Ware.

So like an arrow swift he flew,
  Shot by an archer strong;
So did he fly—which brings me to
  The middle of my song.

Away went Gilpin, out of breath,
  And sore against his will,

Till at his friend the calender's
His horse at last stood still.

The calender, amazed to see
His neighbour in such trim,
Laid down his pipe, flew to the gate.
And thus accosted him:

'What news? what news? your tidings tell;
Tell me you must and shall—
Say why bareheaded you are come,
Or why you come at all?'

Now Gilpin had a pleasant wit,
And loved a timely joke;
And thus unto the calender
In merry guise he spoke:

'I came because your horse would come;
And, if I well forebode,
My hat and wig will soon be here,
They are upon the road.'

The calender, right glad to find
His friend in merry pin,
Returned him not a single word,
But to the house went in;

Whence straight he came with hat and wig,
A wig that flowed behind,
A hat not much the worse for wear,
Each comely in its kind.

He held them up, and in his turn
Thus showed his ready wit:

'My head is twice as big as yours,
  They therefore needs must fit.'

'But let me scrape the dirt away,
  That hangs upon your face;
And stop and eat, for well you may
  Be in a hungry case.'

Said John, 'It is my wedding-day,
  And all the world would stare
If wife should dine at Edmonton,
  And I should dine at Ware.'

So turning to his horse, he said
  'I am in haste to dine;
'Twas for your pleasure you came here,
  You shall go back for mine.'

Ah! luckless speech, and bootless boast!
  For which he paid full dear;
For while he spake, a braying ass
  Did sing most loud and clear;

Whereat his horse did snort, as he
  Had heard a lion roar,
And galloped off with all his might,
  As he had done before.

Away went Gilpin, and away
  Went Gilpin's hat and wig;
He lost them sooner than at first,
  For why?—they were too big.

Now Mistress Gilpin, when she saw
  Her husband posting down

Into the country far away,
  She pulled out half-a-crown;

And thus unto the youth she said
  That drove them to the 'Bell,'
'This shall be yours when you bring back
  My husband safe and well.'

The youth did ride, and soon did meet
  John coming back amain;
Whom in a trice he tried to stop,
  By catching at his rein.

But not performing what he meant,
  And gladly would have done,
The frighted steed he frighted more,
  And made him faster run.

Away went Gilpin, and away
  Went postboy at his heels,
The postboy's horse right glad to miss
  The lumbering of the wheels.

Six gentlemen upon the road,
  Thus seeing Gilpin fly,
With postboy scampering in the rear.
  They raised the hue and cry.

'Stop thief! stop thief! a highwayman!'
  Not one of them was mute;
And all and each that passed that way
  Did join in the pursuit.

And now the turnpike-gates again
  Flew open in short space;

The toll-man thinking, as before,
  That Gilpin rode a race.

And so he did, and won it too,
  For he got first to town;
Nor stopped till where he had got up,
  He did again get down.

Now let us sing, Long live the King,
  And Gilpin, long live he;
And when he next doth ride abroad.
  May I be there to see.

The First Voyage of Sindbad the Sailor

My father was a merchant of high rank and rich possessions. He died when I was but a child, leaving me all his wealth. When I reached manhood's estate I used my inheritance with no thought for the morrow, living in a sumptuous manner and consorting with the richest young men of Baghdad. I continued this life for many years until, at last, when reason prevailed with me to mend my plan, I found with dismay that I had sunk to poverty. And then it was that I arose and sold what goods remained to me for three thousand pieces of silver, and girded myself, resolving to travel to other lands and rebuild my fortune by the wit of my mind and the labour of my hands.

With a part of my hoard I bought merchandise for exchange in far lands, and also such things as I should require in my travels. Thus prepared I set sail with a company of merchants in a ship bound for the city of El-Basrah. For many days and nights we sailed upon the sea, visiting islands and passing thence to other islands; and everywhere we bartered, and bought and sold. At length we came to an island unlike the others. It seemed like a garden that had floated from off the sides of Paradise and established itself in the sea. And here our ship cast anchor and we landed. Then fires were lighted, and, while some cooked, others washed in the cool stream, and yet others amused themselves admiring the beauties of the place.

When all had eaten of the food prepared the shore became a gay scene of sport and play, in which I engaged to the full. But, suddenly, a cry from the master of the ship put an end to our gaiety. Standing at the side of the vessel he called loudly, 'Hear me, and may God preserve you! Hasten back and leave everything; save yourselves from sudden death, for this that ye think is an island is not such. It is a mighty fish lying entranced in sleep on the surface of the sea since times of old, and trees have grown upon it; but your fires and your frolicking have awakened it, and lo! it moves; and, if it sink into the sea, ye will assuredly be drowned. Hasten then, and save yourselves!'

At this we all, with one accord, left everything and fled for the ship, hoping to escape with our lives. While we were making for safety the island moved with a great turmoil and sank behind us in the sea, and the waves leapt against each other above it. For a time I gave myself up as lost, for I was drawn down fathoms deep; but, by God's grace, I rose again to the surface, and to my hand was one of the large wooden bowls which some of the passengers had taken on shore for the purpose of washing. This I seized, and established myself in it, and thus combated the leaping waves, steadying myself with my hands and feet. In vain I called on the master of the ship. He heard me not. He had spread his sails and pursued his way, thinking that none beside those who had been taken up were left alive.

Astride my wooden bowl I gazed longingly at the ship until it was out of sight. Then I prepared for death as the night was closing around me. Perchance I swooned, for I remembered naught else until I found myself stranded upon a mountainous island. There were trees overhanging, and I grasped a drooping bough and drew myself up from the fretting wave. My limbs were benumbed, and, on looking at my legs, I saw the marks made by the nibbling teeth of fish, and marvelled at my salvation from death.

Staggering forward, I flung myself high on the beach like one dead, and so I remained until the dawn of the next day, when the sun, rising upon me, woke me to a sense of such a condition as I had never known before. Long—long it was before I could rise to a sitting posture, and longer still before I could crawl on my hands and knees to a space of grass that was shielded from the sun. Thence, in time, I staggered till I came to a brook, of which I drank; and strength returned to me. I found luscious fruits and ate of them, and drank again of the clear waters of the brook. And so I continued many days roaming the island and wondering at its beauties until I was strong again as before.

And it chanced, as I took my way to and fro in the island, revelling in the sight of things that God had set there, that on a day when the sea was sounding loudly on the shore I beheld something in the distance which excited my curiosity. It seemed like a wild animal of gigantic size, and, as I approached, I feared it was some fabulous beast of the sea. But, as I drew still nearer, I was overcome with amazement to see a beautiful mare standing high, with mane and tail floating on the breeze. She was tethered to a stake on the shore, and, at sight of me, she screamed loudly and stamped her fore-feet on the sand; but, ere I turned to flee, I beheld a man come forth from a cave near by, and he ran after me, calling on me to give an account of myself and my presence in that place. Thereupon I laid my story before him, sparing no detail, even to the wooden bowl by means of which and the grace of God I had come thither.

Gladness seized him at my recital, and he took my hand. Saying, 'Come with me!' he led me into his cave and set food before me. I ate until I was satisfied; and, being at my ease, I repeated my story more minutely, and he wondered thereat. Then I said, 'Thou hast the truth of my adventures upon the sea; now I pray thee, O my master, tell me who *thou* art, that thou dwellest hidden in a cave while thy mare is tethered on the shore.' He was in no way displeased at my curiosity, but answered me in plain words. 'I am one of the grooms of the King El-Mihraj,' he said, 'and the others are scattered about the island. For, look you, friend, it is the time of the new moon, when the sea-horse cometh up out of the sea; and it is our plan to bring our best mares hither and tether them by the shore so that they may lure the sea-horses into our hands.'

While I was wondering at the manner of this cunning device a magnificent sea-horse rose from the waves, shaking the foam from its crest and neighing loudly. As it approached, my companion drew me into the cave and placed himself at the opening with a long coil of thick cord in his hand. Presently by means of this he leashed the sea-horse with great dexterity, and fettered him, and subdued him. Then, with the mare and the sea-horse, he led me to his companions, who, when they had heard my story, were all of one mind that I should accompany them to the city of the King. So they mounted me on one of the mares and I rode with them to the King's palace.

As soon as we had arrived at the palace gates they went in to the King and informed him of my strange adventures; whereupon he sent for me, and they led me before him. He greeted me very courteously and bade me tell him my story, which, when he had heard it, filled him with amazement, so that he cried, 'By Allah! my son, of a truth thou art favoured by fate; for how else could'st thou escape so great a peril? Praise God for thy deliverance!' And he made much of me and caused me to be treated with honour; and he appointed me master of the harbour and comptroller of the shipping.

My condition then was no longer that of a wayfarer. I rose day by day to a higher and a higher place in the King's favour, and he took me into his council in all affairs of State. For a long time I served him well, and he ceased not to recompense me with a liberal hand. Yet my thoughts turned ever to Baghdad, the Abode of Peace; but, when I enquired of merchants and travellers and masters of ships, in which direction it lay, and how one might come at it, they one and all shook their heads at the name of a strange city of which they had never heard. At last, weary of the wonders of that island and the sea around it—wonders of which, if I had time to tell you, would cause you the greatest amazement,—wearied, too, with my arduous duties, but most of all with my prolonged absence from my own land, I stood one day on the sea shore when a great ship drew near and a number of merchants landed from it.

The sailors brought forth their merchandise, and, when I had made an account of it, I enquired of the master of the ship if that were the whole of his cargo. 'All, O my master,' he replied; 'all save some bales whose owner was drowned on our voyage hither; but even these, being in my charge, I desire to sell on behalf of his family in Baghdad.' 'Sayest thou so?' I cried. 'Tell me, I pray thee, the name of the owner of these goods.' And he replied, 'His name was Sindbad the Sailor, and he was drowned on our way hither.'

When I heard this I regarded him more closely and recognized him. Then I cried out, 'O my master, I am he; and they are my goods that are in thy hold.' But he neither recognized me nor believed my words; whereupon I narrated to him the history of my supposed death; but he shook his head and called upon Allah to witness that there was neither faith nor conscience in any. 'Look you!' he said. 'Thou heardst me say the owner was dead, and therefore thou desirest the goods for thyself free of price. I tell thee we saw him sink into the sea with many others.' 'O my master,' I answered, 'hear me and then judge of my veracity.' With this I narrated to him many trivial things which happened before we reached the great-fish island, and which could never be known to me had I not been on the ship. And then it was that he and many of the merchants regarded me with fixed looks and recognized me. 'By Allah!' said they one and all, 'we truly believed thee drowned, but here we find thee alive.' And they pressed upon me and congratulated me, and the master of the ship gave me my goods, at sight of which I was overjoyed; and they all rejoiced with me.

Mindful of the King I served, I at once opened my bales, and, selecting the most costly articles, went in to him and laid them at his feet, telling him how I had regained the goods of which they were a part. And the King wondered greatly at my good fortune and graciously accepted my gifts. He also showed me great favour and honour in that he bestowed upon me gifts in return for mine.

Then, having sold my remaining goods at a profit, I bought largely of the merchandise of the city, and, when the ship was about to sail, I approached the King and thanked him for his great kindness to me, and humbly begged his leave to depart to my own city and family. So he gave me his blessing and a great wealth of merchandise and rare commodities, and bade me farewell. And soon thereafter, having stowed all my goods in the hold of the ship, I set sail with the others for Baghdad.

Our voyage was fortunate, and, with the aid of favourable winds, we reached the city of El-Basrah in safety. Thence I repaired to Baghdad, and my family and my friends gave me a joyous welcome. And when I had sold my merchandise I set up a large establishment, sparing no cost. And I bought land and houses, and gathered round me wealthy companions, in whose society I soon forgot the dangers and terrors I had suffered in other lands. Such is the story of my first voyage; and, to-morrow, by God's grace, I will narrate to you the strange adventures of my second voyage.

The Crescent Moon

RABINDRANATH TAGORE

THE HOME

I paced alone on the road across the field while the sunset was hiding its last gold like a miser.

The daylight sank deeper and deeper into the darkness, and the widowed land, whose harvest had been reaped, lay silent.

Suddenly a boy's shrill voice rose into the sky. He traversed the dark unseen, leaving the track of his song across the hush of the evening.

His village home lay there at the end of the waste land, beyond the sugar-cane field, hidden among the shadows of the banana and the slender areca palm, the cocoa-nut and the dark green jack-fruit trees.

I stopped for a moment in my lonely way under the starlight, and saw spread before me the darkened earth surrounding with her arms countless homes furnished with cradles and beds, mothers' hearts and evening lamps, and young lives glad with a gladness that knows nothing of its value for the world.

ON THE SEASHORE

On the seashore of endless worlds children meet.

The infinite sky is motionless overhead and the restless water is boisterous. On the seashore of endless worlds the children meet with shouts and dances.

They build their houses with sand, and they play with empty shells. With withered leaves they weave their boats and smilingly float them on the vast deep. Children have their play on the seashore of worlds.

They know not how to swim, they know not how to cast nets. Pearl-fishers dive for pearls, merchants sail in their ships, while children gather pebbles and scatter them again. They seek not for hidden treasures, they know not how to cast nets.

The sea surges up with laughter, and pale gleams the smile of the sea-beach. Death-dealing waves sing meaningless ballads to the children, even like a mother while rocking her baby's cradle. The sea plays with children, and pale gleams the smile of the sea-beach.

On the seashore of endless worlds children meet. Tempest roams in the pathless sky, ships are wrecked in the trackless water, death is abroad and children play. On the seashore of endless worlds is the great meeting of children.

THE SOURCE

The sleep that flits on baby's eyes—does anybody know from where it comes? Yes, there is a rumour that it has its dwelling where, in the fairy village among shadows of the forest dimly lit with glow-worms, there hang two shy buds of enchantment. From there it comes to kiss baby's eyes.

The smile that flickers on baby's lips when he sleeps—does anybody know where it was born? Yes, there is a rumour that a young pale beam of a crescent moon touched the edge of a vanishing autumn cloud, and there the smile was first born in the dream of a dew-washed morning—the smile that flickers on baby's lips when he sleeps.

The sweet, soft freshness that blooms on baby's limbs—does anybody know where it was hidden so long? Yes, when the mother was a young girl it lay pervading her heart in tender and silent mystery of love—the sweet, soft freshness that has bloomed on baby's limbs.

BABY'S WAY

If baby only wanted to, he could fly up to heaven this moment.

It is not for nothing that he does not leave us.

He loves to rest his head on mother's bosom, and cannot ever bear to lose sight of her.

Baby knows all manner of wise words, though few on earth can understand their meaning.

It is not for nothing that he never wants to speak.

The one thing he wants is to learn mother's words from mother's lips. That is why he looks so innocent.

Baby had a heap of gold and pearls, yet he came like a beggar on to this earth.

It is not for nothing he came in such a disguise.

This dear little naked mendicant pretends to be utterly helpless, so that he may beg for mother's wealth of love.

Baby was so free from every tie in the land of the tiny crescent moon.

It was not for nothing he gave up his freedom.

He knows that there is room for endless joy in mother's little corner of a heart, and it is sweeter far than liberty to be caught and pressed in her dear arms.

Baby never knew how to cry. He dwelt in the land of perfect bliss.

It is not for nothing he has chosen to shed tears.

Though with the smile of his dear face he draws mother's yearning heart to him, yet his little cries over tiny troubles weave the double bond of pity and love.

THE UNHEEDED PAGEANT

Ah, who was it coloured that little frock, my child, and covered your sweet limbs with that little red tunic?

You have come out in the morning to play in the courtyard, tottering and tumbling as you run.

But who was it coloured that little frock, my child?

What is it makes you laugh, my little life-bud?

Mother smiles at you standing on the threshold.

She claps her hands and her bracelets jingle, and you dance with your bamboo stick in your hand like a tiny little shepherd.

But what is it makes you laugh, my little life-bud?

O beggar, what do you beg for, clinging to your mother's neck with both your hands?

O greedy heart, shall I pluck the world like a fruit from the sky to place it on your little rosy palm?

O beggar, what are you begging for?

The wind carries away in glee the tinkling of your anklet bells.

The sun smiles and watches your toilet. The sky watches over you when you sleep in your mother's arms, and the morning comes tiptoe to your bed and kisses your eyes.

The wind carries away in glee the tinkling of your anklet bells.

The fairy mistress of dreams is coming towards you, flying through the twilight sky.

The world-mother keeps her seat by you in your mother's heart.

He who plays his music to the stars is standing at your window with his flute.

And the fairy mistress of dreams is coming towards you, flying through the twilight sky.

SLEEP-STEALER

Who stole sleep from baby's eyes? I must know.

Clasping her pitcher to her waist mother went to fetch water from the village near by.

It was noon. The children's playtime was over; the ducks in the pond were silent.

The shepherd boy lay asleep under the shadow of the *banyan* tree.

The crane stood grave and still in the swamp near the mango grove.

In the meanwhile the Sleep-stealer came and, snatching sleep from baby's eyes, flew away.

When mother came back she found baby travelling the room over on all fours.

Who stole sleep from our baby's eyes? I must know. I must find her and chain her up.

I must look into that dark cave, where, through boulders and scowling stones, trickles a tiny stream.

I must search in the drowsy shade of the *bakula* grove, where pigeons coo in their corner, and fairies' anklets tinkle in the stillness of starry nights.

In the evening I will peep into the whispering silence of the bamboo forest, where fireflies squander their light, and will ask every creature I meet, 'Can anybody tell me where the Sleep-stealer lives?'

Who stole sleep from baby's eyes? I must know.

Shouldn't I give her a good lesson if I could only catch her!

I would raid her nest and see where she hoards all her stolen sleep.

I would plunder it all, and carry it home.

I would bind her two wings securely, set her on the bank of the river, and then let her play at fishing with a reed among the rushes and water-lilies.

When the marketing is over in the evening, and the village children sit in their mothers' laps, then the night birds will mockingly din her ears with:

'Whose sleep will you steal now?'

THE BEGINNING

'Where have I come from, where did you pick me up?' the baby asked its mother.

She answered half crying, half laughing, and clasping the baby to her breast,—

'You were hidden in my heart as its desire, my darling.

You were in the dolls of my childhood's games; and when with clay I made the image of my god every morning, I made and unmade you then.

You were enshrined with our household deity, in his worship I worshipped you.

In all my hopes and my loves, in my life, in the life of my mother you have lived.

In the lap of the deathless Spirit who rules our home you have been nursed for ages.

When in girlhood my heart was opening its petals, you hovered as a fragrance about it.

Your tender softness bloomed in my youthful limbs, like a glow in the sky before the sunrise.

Heaven's first darling, twin-born with the morning light, you have floated down the stream of the world's life, and at last you have stranded on my heart.

As I gaze on your face, mystery overwhelms me; you who belong to all have become mine.

For fear of losing you I hold you tight to my breast. What magic has snared the world's treasure in these slender arms of mine?'

BABY'S WORLD

I wish I could take a quiet corner in the heart of my baby's very own world.

I know it has stars that talk to him, and a sky that stoops down to his face to amuse him with its silly clouds and rainbows.

Those who make believe to be dumb, and look as if they never could move, come creeping to his window with their stories and with trays crowded with bright toys.

I wish I could travel by the road that crosses baby's mind, and out beyond all bounds;

Where messengers run errands for no cause between the kingdoms of kings of no history;

Where Reason makes kites of her laws and flies them, and Truth sets Fact free from its fetters.

WHEN AND WHY

When I bring you coloured toys, my child, I understand why there is such a play of colours on clouds, on water, and why flowers are painted in tints—when I give coloured toys to you, my child.

When I sing to make you dance, I truly know why there is music in leaves, and why waves send their chorus of voices to the heart of the listening earth—when I sing to make you dance.

When I bring sweet things to your greedy hands, I know why there is honey in the cup of the flower, and why fruits are secretly filled with sweet juice—when I bring sweet things to your greedy hands.

When I kiss your face to make you smile, my darling, I surely understand what pleasure streams from the sky in morning light, and what delight the summer breeze brings to my body—when I kiss you to make you smile.

THE HERO

Mother, let us imagine we are travelling, and passing through a strange and dangerous country.

You are riding in a palanquin and I am trotting by you on a red horse.

It is evening and the sun goes down. The waste of *Joradighi* lies wan and grey before us. The land is desolate and barren.

You are frightened and thinking—'I know not where we have come to.'

I say to you, 'Mother, do not be afraid.'

The meadow is prickly with spiky grass, and through it runs a narrow broken path.

There are no cattle to be seen in the wide field; they have gone to their village stalls.

It grows dark and dim on the land and sky, and we cannot tell where we are going.

Suddenly you call me and ask me in a whisper, 'What light is that near the bank?'

Just then there bursts out a fearful yell, and figures come running towards us.

You sit crouched in your palanquin and repeat the names of the gods in prayer.

The bearers, shaking in terror, hide themselves in the thorny bush.

I shout to you, 'Don't be afraid, mother. I am here.'

With long sticks in their hands and hair all wild about their heads, they come nearer and nearer.

I shout, 'Have a care! you villains! One step more and you are dead men.'

They give another terrible yell and rush forward.

You clutch my hand and say, 'Dear boy, for heaven's sake, keep away from them.'

I say, 'Mother, just you watch me.'

Then I spur my horse for a wild gallop, and my sword and buckler clash against each other.

The fight becomes so fearful, mother, that it would give you a cold shudder could you see it from your palanquin.

Many of them fly, and a great number are cut to pieces.

I know you are thinking, sitting all by yourself, that your boy must be dead by this time.

But I come to you all stained with blood, and say, 'Mother, the fight is over now.'

You come out and kiss me, pressing me to your heart, and you say to yourself, 'I don't know what I should do if I hadn't my boy to escort me.'

A thousand useless things happen day after day, and why couldn't such a thing come true by chance?

It would be like a story in a book.

My brother would say, 'Is it possible? I always thought he was so delicate!'

Our village people would all say in amazement, 'Was it not lucky that the boy was with his mother?'

William Goes to the Pictures

RICHARD CROMPTON

It all began with William's aunt, who was in a good temper that morning, and gave him a shilling for posting a letter for her and carrying her parcels from the grocer's.

'Buy some sweets or go to the Pictures,' she said carelessly, as she gave it to him.

William walked slowly down the road, gazing thoughtfully at the coin. After deep calculations, based on the fact that a shilling is the equivalent of two sixpences, he came to the conclusion that both luxuries could be indulged in.

In the matter of sweets, William frankly upheld the superiority of quantity over quality. Moreover, he knew every sweet shop within a two miles radius of his home whose proprietor added an extra sweet after the scale had descended, and he patronized these shops exclusively. With solemn face and eager eye, he always watched the process of weighing, and 'stingy' shops were known and banned by him.

He wandered now to his favourite confectioner and stood outside the window for five minutes, torn between the rival attractions of Gooseberry Eyes and Marble Balls. Both were sold at 4 ounces for 2d. William never purchased more expensive luxuries. At last his frowning brow relaxed and he entered the shop.

'Sixpennoth of Gooseberry Eyes,' he said, with a slightly self-conscious air. The extent of his purchases rarely exceeded a penny.

'Hello!' said the shopkeeper, in amused surprise.

'Gotter bit of money this mornin,' explained William carelessly, with the air of a Rothschild.

He watched the weighing of the emerald green dainties with silent intensity, saw with satisfaction the extra one added after the scale had fallen, received the precious paper bag, and, putting two sweets into his mouth, walked out of the shop.

Sucking slowly, he walked down the road towards the Picture Palace. William was not in the habit of frequenting Picture Palaces. He had only been there once before in his life.

It was a thrilling programme. First came the story of desperate crooks who, on coming out of any building, glanced cautiously up and down the street in huddled, crouching attitudes, then crept ostentatiously on their way in a manner guaranteed to attract attention and suspicion at any place and time. The plot was involved. They were pursued by police, they leapt on to a moving train and then, for no accountable reason, leapt from that on to a moving motor-car and from that they plunged into a moving river. It was thrilling and William thrilled. Sitting quite motionless, he watched, with wide, fascinated eyes, though his jaws never ceased their rotatory movement and every now and then his hand would go mechanically to the paper bag on his knees and convey a Gooseberry Eye to his mouth.

The next play was a simple country love-story, in which figured a simple country maiden wooed by the squire, who was marked out as the villain by his moustachios.

After many adventures the simple country maiden was won by a simple country son of the soil in picturesque rustic attire, whose emotions were faithfully portrayed by gestures that must have required much gymnastic skill; the villain was finally shown languishing in a prison cell, still indulging in frequent eye-brow play.

Next came another love-story—this time of a noble-hearted couple, consumed with mutual passion and kept apart not only by a series of misunderstandings possible only in a picture play, but also by maidenly pride and reserve on the part of the heroine and manly pride and reserve on the part of the hero that forced them to hide their ardour beneath a cold and haughty exterior. The heroine's brother moved through the story like a good fairy, tender and protective towards his orphan sister and ultimately explained to each the burning passion of the other.

It was moving and touching and William was moved and touched.

The next was a comedy. It began by a solitary workman engaged upon the re-painting of a door and ended with a miscellaneous crowd of people, all covered with paint, falling downstairs on top of one another. It was amusing. William was riotously and loudly amused.

Lastly came the pathetic story of a drunkard's downward path. He began as a wild young man in evening clothes drinking intoxicants and playing cards, he ended as a wild old man in rags still drinking intoxicants and playing cards. He had a small child with a pious and superior expression, who spent her time weeping over him and exhorting him to a better life, till, in a moment of justifiable exasperation, he threw a beer bottle at her head. He then bedewed her bed in Hospital with penitent tears, tore out his hair, flung up his arms towards Heaven, beat his waistcoat, and clasped her to his breast, so that it was not to be wondered at that, after all that excitement, the child had a relapse and with the words 'Good-bye, Father. Do not think of what you have done. I forgive you,' passed peacefully away.

William drew a deep breath at the end, and still sucking, arose with the throng and passed out.

Once outside, he glanced cautiously around and slunk down the road in the direction of his home. Then he doubled suddenly and ran down a back street to put his imaginary pursuers off his track. He took a pencil from his pocket and, levelling it at the empty air, fired twice. Two of his pursuers fell dead, the rest came on with redoubled vigour. There was no time to be lost. Running for dear life, he dashed down the next street, leaving in his wake an elderly gentleman nursing his toe and cursing volubly. As he neared his gate, William again drew the pencil from his pocket and, still looking back down the road, and firing as he went, he rushed into his own gateway.

William's father, who had stayed at home that day because of a bad headache and a touch of liver, picked himself up from the middle of a rhododendron bush and seized William by the back of his neck.

'You young ruffian,' he roared, 'what do you mean by charging into me like that?'

William gently disengaged himself.

'I wasn't chargin', Father,' he said, meekly. 'I was only jus' comin' in at the gate, same as other folks. I jus' wasn't looking jus' the way you were coming, but I can't look all ways at once, cause——'

'Be quiet!' roared William's father.

Like the rest of the family, he dreaded William's eloquence.

'What's that on your tongue! Put your tongue out.'

William obeyed. The colour of William's tongue would have put to shame Spring's freshest tints.

'How many times am I to tell you,' bellowed William's father, 'that I won't have you going about eating filthy poisons all day between meals?'

'It's not filthy poison,' said William. 'It's jus' a few sweets Aunt Susan gave me 'cause I kin'ly went to the post office for her an'——'

'Be quiet! Have you got any more of the foul things?'

'They're not foul things,' said William, doggedly. 'They're good. Jus' have one, an' try. They're jus' a few sweets Aunt Susan kin'ly gave me an'——'

'Be quiet! Where are they?'

Slowly and reluctantly William drew forth his bag. His father seized it and flung it far into the bushes. For the next ten minutes William conducted a thorough and systematic search among the bushes and for the rest of the day consumed Gooseberry Eyes and garden soil in fairly equal proportions.

He wandered round to the back garden and climbed on to the wall.

'Hello!' said the little girl next door, looking up.

Something about the little girl's head and curls reminded William of the simple country maiden. There was a touch of the artistic temperament about William. He promptly felt himself the simple country son of the soil.

'Hullo, Joan,' he said in a deep, husky voice intended to be expressive of intense affection. 'Have you missed me while I've been away?'

'Didn't know you'd been away,' said Joan. 'What are you talking so funny for?'

'I'm not talkin' funny,' said William in the same husky voice, 'I can't help talkin' like this.'

'You've got a cold. That's what you've got. That's what Mother said when she saw you splashing about with your rain tub this morning.' She said, 'The next thing that we shall hear of William Brown will be he's in bed with a cold.'

'It's not a cold,' said William mysteriously. 'It's jus' the way I feel.'

'What are you eating?'

'Gooseberry Eyes. Like one?' He took the packet from his pocket and handed it down to her. 'Go on. Take two—three,' he said in reckless generosity.

'But they're—dirty.'

'Go on. It's only ord'nery dirt. It soon sucks off. They're jolly good.' He poured a shower of them lavishly down to her.

'I say,' he said, reverting to his character of simple country lover. 'Did you say you'd missed me? I bet you didn't think of me as much as I did of you. I jus' bet you didn't.' His voice had sunk deeper and deeper till it almost died away.

'I say, William, does your throat hurt you awful, that you've got to talk like that?'

Her blue eyes were anxious and sympathetic.

William put one hand to his throat and frowned.

'A bit,' he confessed lightly.

'Oh, William!' she clasped her hands. 'Does it hurt all the time?'

Her solicitude was flattering.

'I don't talk much about it, anyway, do I?' he said manfully.

She started up and stared at him with big blue eyes.

'Oh, William! Is it—is it your—lungs? I've got an aunt that's got lungs and she coughs and coughs,' William coughed hastily, 'and it hurts her and makes her awful bad. Oh, William, I do hope you've not got lungs.'

Her tender, anxious little face was upturned to him. 'I guess

I have got lungs,' he said, 'but I don't make a fuss about 'em.'

He coughed again.

'What does the doctor say about it?'

William considered a minute.

'He says it's lungs all right,' he said at last. 'He says I gotter be jolly careful.'

'William, would you like my new paintbox?'

'I don't think so. Not now. Thanks.'

'I've got three balls and one's quite new. Wouldn't you like it, William?'

'No—thanks. You see, it's no use my collectin' a lot of things. You never know—with lungs.'

'Oh, William!'

Her distress was pathetic.

'Of course,' he said hastily, 'if I'm careful it'll be all right. Don't you worry about me.'

'Joan!' from the house.

'That's Mother. Good-bye, William dear. If Father brings me home any chocolate, I'll bring it in to you. I will—honest. Thanks for the Gooseberry Eyes. Good-bye.'

'Good-bye—and don't worry about me,' he added bravely.

He put another Gooseberry Eye into his mouth and wandered round aimlessly to the front of the house. His grown-up sister, Ethel, was at the front door, shaking hands with a young man.

'I'll do all I can for you,' she was saying earnestly.

Their hands were clasped.

'I know you will,' he said equally earnestly.

Both look and handclasp were long. The young man walked away. Ethel stood at the door, gazing after him, with a far-away look in her eyes. William was interested.

'That was Jack Morgan, wasn't it?' he said.

'Yes,' said Ethel absently and went into the house.

The look, the long handclasp, the words lingered in William's memory. They must be jolly fond of each other, like people are when they're engaged, but he knew they weren't engaged. P'raps they were too proud to let each other know how fond they were of each other—like the man and girl at the pictures. Ethel wanted a brother like the one in the pictures to let the man know she was fond of him. Then a light came suddenly into William's mind and he stood, deep in thought.

Inside the drawing-room, Ethel was talking to her mother.

'He's going to propose to her next Sunday. He told me about it because I'm her best friend, and he wanted to ask me if I thought he'd any chance. I said I thought he had, and I said I'd try and prepare her a little and put in a good word for him if I could. Isn't it thrilling?'

'Yes, dear. By the way, did you see William anywhere? I do hope he's not in mischief.'

'He was in the front garden a minute ago.' She went to the window. 'He's not there now, though.'

William had just arrived at Mr Morgan's house.

The maid showed him into Mr Morgan's sitting-room.

'Mr Brown,' she announced.

The young man rose to receive his guest with politeness not unmixed with bewilderment. His acquaintance with William was of the slightest.

'Good afternoon,' said William. 'I've come from Ethel.'

'Yes?'

'Yes.' William fumbled in his pocket and at last drew forth a rosebud, slightly crushed by its close confinement in the company of the Gooseberry Eyes, a penknife, a top and a piece of putty.

'She sent you this,' said William gravely.

Mr Morgan gazed at it with the air of one who is sleep-walking.

'Yes? Er—very kind of her.'

'Kinder keep-sake. Souveneer,' explained William.

'Yes. Er—any message?'

'Oh, yes. She wants you to come in and see her this evening.'

'Er—yes. Of course. I've just come from her. Perhaps she remembered something she wanted to tell me after I'd gone.'

'P'raps.'

Then, 'Any particular time?'

'No. 'Bout seven, I expect.'

'Oh, yes.'

Mr Morgan's eyes were fixed with a fascinated wondering gaze upon the limp, and by no means spotless, rose-bud.

'You say she—sent this?'

'Yes.'

'And no other message?'

'No.'

'Er—well, say I'll come with pleasure, will you?'

'Yes.'

Silence.

Then, 'She thinks an awful lot of you, Ethel does.'

Mr Morgan passed a hand over his brow.

'Yes? Kind—er—very kind, I'm sure.'

'Always talkin' about you in her sleep,' went on William, warming to his theme. 'I sleep in the next room and I can hear her talkin' about you all night. Jus' sayin' your name over and over again. "Jack Morgan, Jack Morgan, Jack Morgan".' William's voice was husky and soulful. 'Jus' like that—over an' over again. "Jack Morgan, Jack Morgan, Jack Morgan."'

Mr Morgan was speechless. He sat gazing with horror-stricken face at his young visitor.

'Are you—sure?' he said at last. 'It might be someone else's name.'

'No, 'tisn't,' said William firmly. 'It's yours. "Jack Morgan, Jack Morgan, Jack Morgan"—jus' like that. An' she eats just nothin' now. Always hangin' round the windows to watch you pass.'

The perspiration stood out in beads on Mr Morgan's brow.

'It's—horrible,' he said at last in a hoarse whisper.

William was gratified. The young man had at last realized his cruelty. But William never liked to leave a task half done. He still sat on and calmly and silently considered his next statement. Mechanically he put a hand into his pocket and conveyed a Gooseberry Eye to his mouth. Mr Morgan also sat in silence with a stricken look upon his face, gazing into vacancy.

'She's got your photo,' said William at last, 'fixed up into one of those little round things on a chain round her neck.'

'Are—you—sure?' said Mr Morgan desperately.

'Sure's fate,' said William rising. 'Well, I'd better be goin'. She pertic-ler wants to see you alone to-night. Good-bye.'

But Mr Morgan did not answer. He sat huddled up in his chair staring in front of him long after William had gone jauntily on his way. Then he moistened his dry lips.

'Good Lord,' he groaned.

William was thinking of the pictures as he went home. That painter one was jolly good. When they all got all over paint! And when they all fell downstairs! William suddenly guffawed out loud at the memory. But what had the painter chap been doing at the very beginning before he began to paint? He'd been getting off the old paint with a sort of torch thing and a knife, then he began putting the new paint on. Just sort of melting the old paint and then scraping it off. William had never seen it done in real life, but he supposed that was the way you did get old paint off. Melting it with some sort of fire, then scraping it off. He wasn't sure whether it was that, but he could find out. As he entered the house he took his penknife from his pocket, opened it thoughtfully, and went upstairs.

Mr Brown came home about dinner-time.

'How's your head, father?' said Ethel sympathetically.

'Rotten!' said Mr Brown, sinking wearily into an arm-chair.

'Perhaps dinner will do it good,' said Mrs Brown, 'it ought to be ready now.'

The housemaid entered the room.

'Mr Morgan, mam. He wants to see Miss Ethel. I've shown him into the library.'

'Now?' exploded Mr Brown. 'What the deu—why the dickens is the young idiot coming at this time of day? Seven o'clock! What time does he think we have dinner? What does he mean by coming round paying calls on people at dinner time? What——'

'Ethel, dear,' interrupted Mrs Brown, 'do go and see what he wants and get rid of him as soon as you can.'

Ethel entered the library, carefully closing the door behind her to keep out the sound of her father's comments, which were plainly audible across the hall.

She noticed something wan and haggard-looking on Mr Morgan's face as he rose to greet her.

'Er—good evening, Miss Brown.'

'Good evening, Mr Morgan.'

Then they sat in silence, both awaiting some explanation of the visit. The silence became oppressive. Mr Morgan, with an air of acute misery and embarrassment, shifted his feet and coughed. Ethel looked at the clock. Then—

'Was it raining when you came, Mr Morgan?'

'Raining? Er—no. No—not at all.'

Silence.

'I thought it looked like rain this afternoon.'

'Yes, of course. Er—no, not at all.'

Silence.

'It does make the roads so bad round here when it rains.'

'Yes.' Mr Morgan put up a hand as though to loosen his collar. 'Er—very bad.'

'Almost impassable.'

'Er—quite.'

Silence again.

Inside the drawing-room, Mr Brown was growing restive. 'Is dinner to be kept waiting for that youth all night? Quarter past seven! You know it's just what I can't stand—having my meals interfered with. Is my digestion to be ruined simply because this young nincompoop chooses to pay his social calls at seven o'clock at night?'

'Then we must ask him to dinner,' said Mrs Brown, desperately. 'We really must.'

'We must not,' said Mr Brown. 'Can't I stay away from the office for one day with a headache, without having to entertain all the young jackasses for miles around.' The telephone bell rang. He raised his hands above his head.

'Oh——'

'I'll go, dear,' said Mrs Brown hastily.

She returned with a worried frown on her brow.

'It's Mrs Clive,' she said. 'She says Joan has been very sick because of some horrible sweets William gave her, and she said she was so sorry to hear about William and hoped he'd be better soon. I couldn't quite make it out, but it seems that William has been telling them that he had to go and see a doctor about his lungs and the doctor said they were very weak and he'd have to be careful.'

Mr Brown sat up and looked at her. 'But—why—on—earth?' he said slowly.

'I don't know, dear,' said Mrs Brown, helplessly. 'I don't know anything about it.'

'He's mad,' said Mr Brown with conviction. 'Mad. It's the only explanation.'

Then came the opening and shutting of the front door and Ethel entered. She was very flushed.

'He's gone,' she said. 'Mother, it's simply horrible! He didn't tell me much, but it seems that William actually went to his house and told him that I wanted to see him alone at seven o'clock this evening. I've hardly spoken to William to-day. He couldn't have misunderstood anything I said. And he actually took a flower with him—a dreadful-looking rosebud—and said I'd sent it. I simply didn't know where to look or what to say. It was horrible!'

Mrs Brown sat gazing weakly at her daughter.

Mr Brown rose with the air of a man goaded beyond endurance.

'Where is William?' he said shortly.

'I don't know, but I thought I heard him go upstairs some time ago.'

William was upstairs. For the last twenty minutes he had been happily and quietly engaged upon his bedroom door with a lighted taper in one hand and penknife in the other. There was no doubt about it. By successful experiment he had proved that that was the way you got old paint off. When Mr Brown came upstairs he had entirely stripped one panel of its paint.

Kaa's Hunting

RUDYARD KIPLING

All that is told here happened some time before Mowgli was turned out of the Seeonee wolf-pack. It was in the days when Baloo was teaching him the Law of the Jungle. The big, serious, old brown bear was delighted to have so quick a pupil, for the young wolves will only learn as much of the Law of the Jungle as applies to their own pack and tribe, and run away as soon as they can repeat the Hunting Verse: 'Feet that make no noise; eyes that can see in the dark; ears that can hear the winds in their lairs, and sharp white teeth—all these things are the marks of our brothers except Tabaqui and the Hyena, whom we hate.' But Mowgli, as a man-cub, had to learn a great deal more than this. Sometimes Bagheera, the Black Panther, would come lounging through the jungle to see how his pet was getting on, and would purr with his head against a tree while Mowgli recited the day's lesson to Baloo. The boy could climb almost as well as he could swim, and swim almost as well as he could run; so Baloo, the Teacher of the Law, taught him the Wood and Water laws: how to tell a rotten branch from a sound one; how to speak politely to the wild bees when he came upon a hive of them fifty feet aboveground; what to say to Mang, the Bat, when he disturbed him in the branches at midday; and how to warn the water-snakes in the pools before he splashed down among them. None of the Jungle People like being disturbed, and all are very ready to fly at an intruder. Then, too, Mowgli was taught the Strangers' Hunting Call, which must be repeated aloud till it is answered, whenever one of the Jungle People hunts outside his own grounds. It means, translated: 'Give me leave to hunt here because I am hungry'; and the answer is: 'Hunt, then, for food, but not for pleasure.'

All this will show you how much Mowgli had to learn by heart, and he grew very tired of repeating the same thing a hundred times; but, as Baloo said to Bagheera one day when Mowgli had been cuffed and had run off in a temper: 'A man's cub is a man's cub, and he must learn *all* the Law of the Jungle.'

'But think how small he is,' said the Black Panther, who would have spoiled Mowgli if he had had his own way. 'How can his little head carry all thy long talk?'

'Is there anything in the jungle too little to be killed? No. That is why I teach him these things, and that is why I hit him, very softly, when he forgets.'

'Softly! What dost thou know of softness, old Iron-feet?' Bagheera grunted. 'His face is all bruised to-day by thy—softness. Ugh!'

'Better he should be bruised from head to foot by me who love him than that he should come to harm through ignorance,' Baloo answered, very earnestly. 'I am now teaching him the Master Words of the Jungle that shall protect him with the Birds and the Snake People, and all that hunt on four feet, except his own pack. He can now claim protection, if he will only remember the Words, from all in the jungle. Is not that worth a little beating?'

'Well, look to it then that thou dost not kill the man-cub. He is no tree-trunk to sharpen thy blunt claws upon. But what are those Master Words? I am more likely to give help than to ask it'—Bagheera stretched out one paw and admired the steel-blue ripping-chisel talons at the end of it—'Still I should like to know.'

'I will call Mowgli and he shall say then—if he will. Come, Little Brother!'

'My head is ringing like a bee-tree,' said a sullen voice over their heads, and Mowgli slid down a tree-trunk, very angry and indignant, adding, as he reached the ground: 'I come for Bagheera and not for *thee*, fat old Baloo!'

'That is all one to me,' said Baloo, though he was hurt and grieved. 'Tell Bagheera, then, the Master Words of the Jungle that I have taught thee this day.'

'Master Words for which people?' said Mowgli, delighted to show off. 'The jungle has many tongues. *I* know them all.'

'A little thou knowest, but not much. See, O Bagheera, they never thank their teacher! Not one small wolfling has come back to thank old Baloo for his teachings. Say the Word for the Hunting People, then, great scholar!'

'We be of one blood, ye and I,' said Mowgli, giving the words the Bear accent which all the Hunting People of the Jungle use.

'Good! Now for the Birds.'

Mowgli repeated, with the Kite's whistle at the end of the sentence.

'Now for the Snake People,' said Bagheera.

The answer was a perfectly indescribable hiss, and Mowgli kicked up his feet behind, clapped his hands together to applaud himself, and jumped on Bagheera's back, where he sat sideways, drumming with his heels on the glossy skin and making the worst faces that he could think of at Baloo.

'There—there! That was worth a little bruise,' said the Brown Bear, tenderly. 'Some day thou wilt remember me.' Then he turned aside to tell Bagheera how he had begged the Master Words from Hathi, the Wild Elephant, who knows all about these things, and how Hathi had taken Mowgli down to a pool to get the Snake Word from a water-snake, because Baloo could not pronounce it, and how Mowgli was now reasonably safe against all accidents in the jungle, because neither snake, bird, nor beast would hurt him.

'No one then is to be feared,' Baloo wound up, patting his big furry stomach with pride.

'Except his own tribe,' said Bagheera, under his breath; and then aloud to Mowgli: 'Have a care for my ribs, Little Brother! What is all this dancing up and down?'

Mowgli had been trying to make himself heard by pulling at Bagheera's shoulder-fur and kicking hard. When the two listened to him he was shouting at the top of his voice: 'And *so* I shall have a tribe of my own, and lead them through the branches all day long.'

'What is this new folly, little dreamer of dreams?' said Bagheera.

'Yes, and throw branches and dirt at old Baloo,' Mowgli went on. 'They have promised me this, ah!'

'Whoof!' Baloo's big paw scooped Mowgli off Bagheera's back, and as the boy lay between the big fore paws he could see the bear was angry.

'Mowgli,' said Baloo, 'thou hast been talking with the Bandar-log—the Monkey People.'

Mowgli looked at Bagheera to see if the panther was angry too, and Bagheera's eyes were as hard as jade-stones.

'Thou hast been with the Monkey People—the gray apes—

the people without a Law—the eaters of everything. That is great shame.'

'When Baloo hurt my head,' said Mowgli (he was still down on his back), 'I went away, and the gray apes came down from the trees and had pity on me. No one else cared.' He snuffled a little.

'The pity of the Monkey People!' Baloo snorted.

'The stillness of the mountain stream! The cool of the summer sun! And then, man-cub?'

'And then—and then they gave me nuts and pleasant things to eat, and they—they carried me in their arms up to the top of the trees and said I was their blood-brother, except that I had no tail, and should be their leader some day.'

'They have *no* leader,' said Bagheera. 'They lie. They have always lied.'

'They were very kind, and bade me come again. Why have I never been taken among the Monkey People? They stand on their feet as I do. They do not hit me with hard paws. They play all day. Let me get up! Bad Baloo, let me up! I will go play with them again.'

'Listen, man-cub,' said the bear, and his voice rumbled like thunder on a hot night. 'I have taught thee all the Law of the Jungle for all the Peoples of the Jungle—except the Monkey Folk who live in the trees. They have no Law. They are outcastes. They have no speech of their own, but use the stolen words which they overhear when they listen and peep and wait up above in the branches. Their way is not our way. They are without leaders. They have no remembrance. They boast and chatter and pretend that they are a great people about to do great affairs in the jungle, but the falling of a nut turns their minds to laughter, and all is forgotten. We of the jungle have no dealings with them. We do not drink where the monkeys drink; we do not go where the monkeys go; we do not hunt where they hunt; we do not die where they die. Hast thou ever heard me speak of the Bandar-log till to-day?'

'No,' said Mowgli in a whisper, for the forest was very still now that Baloo had finished.

'The Jungle People put them out of their mouths and out of their minds. They are very many, evil, dirty, shameless, and they desire, if they have any fixed desire, to be noticed by the Jungle People. But we do *not* notice them even when they throw nuts and filth on our heads.'

He had hardly spoken when a shower of nuts and twigs spattered down through the branches; and they could hear coughings and howlings and angry jumpings high up in the air among the thin branches.

'The Monkey People are forbidden,' said Baloo, 'forbidden to the Jungle People. Remember.'

'Forbidden,' said Bagheera; 'but I still think Baloo should have warned thee against them.'

'I—I? How was I to guess he would play with such dirt. The Monkey People! Faugh!'

A fresh shower came down on their heads, and the two trotted away, taking Mowgli with them. What Baloo had said about the monkeys was perfectly true. They belonged to the tree-tops, and as beasts very seldom look up, there was no occasion for the monkeys and the Jungle People to cross one another's path. But whenever they found a sick wolf, or a wounded tiger or bear, the monkeys would torment him, and would throw sticks and nuts at any beast for fun and in the hope of being noticed. Then they would howl and shriek senseless songs, and invite the Jungle People to climb up their trees and fight them, or would start furious battles over nothing among themselves, and leave the dead monkeys where the Jungle People could see them.

They were always just going to have a leader and laws and customs of their own, but they never did, because their memories would not hold over from day to day, and so they settled things by making up a saying: 'What the Bandar-log think now the Jungle will think later'; and that comforted them a great deal. None of the beasts could reach them, but on the other hand none of the beasts would notice them, and that was why they were so pleased when Mowgli came to play with them, and when they heard how angry Baloo was.

They never meant to do any more—the Bandar-log never mean anything at all—but one of them invented what seemed to him a brilliant idea, and he told all the others that Mowgli would be a useful person to keep in the tribe, because he could weave sticks together for protection from the wind; so, if they caught him, they could make him teach them. Of course Mowgli, as a wood-cutter's child, inherited all sorts of instincts, and used to make little play-huts of fallen branches without thinking how he came to do it. The Monkey People, watching in the trees, considered these huts most wonderful. This time, they said, they were really going to have a leader and become the wisest people in the jungle—so wise that every one else would notice and envy them. Therefore they followed Baloo and Bagheera and Mowgli through the jungle very quietly till it was time for the midday nap, and Mowgli, who was very much ashamed of himself, slept between the panther and the bear, resolving to have no more to do with the Monkey People.

The next thing he remembered was feeling hands on his legs and arms—hard, strong little hands—and then a swash of branches in his face; and then he was staring down through the swaying boughs as Baloo woke the jungle with his deep cries and Bagheera bounded up the trunk with every tooth bared. The Bandar-log howled with triumph, and scuffled away to the upper branches where Bagheera dared not follow, shouting: 'He has noticed us! Bagheera has noticed us! All the Jungle People admire us for our skill and our cunning!' Then they began their flight; and the flight of the Monkey People through tree-land is one of the things nobody can describe. They have their regular roads and cross-roads, uphills and downhills, all laid out from fifty to seventy or a hundred feet aboveground, and by these they can travel even at night if necessary.

Two of the strongest monkeys caught Mowgli under the arms and swung off with him through the tree-tops, twenty feet at a bound. Had they been alone they could have gone twice as fast, but the boy's weight held them back. Sick and giddy as Mowgli was he could not help enjoying the wild rush, though the glimpses of earth far down below frightened him, and the terrible check and jerk at the end of the swing over nothing but empty air brought his heart between his teeth.

His escort would rush him up a tree till he felt the weak topmost branches crackle and bend under them, and, then, with a cough and a whoop, would fling themselves into the air outward and downward, and bring up hanging by their hands or their feet to the lower limbs of the next tree. Sometimes he could see for miles and miles over the still green jungle, as a man on the top of a mast can see for miles across the sea, and then the branches and leaves would lash him across the face, and he and his two guards would be almost down to earth again.

So bounding and crashing and whooping and yelling, the

whole tribe of Bandar-log swept along the tree-roads with Mowgli their prisoner.

For a time he was afraid of being dropped; then he grew angry, but he knew better than to struggle; and then he began to think. The first thing was to send back word to Baloo and Bagheera, for, at the pace the monkeys were going, he knew his friends would be left far behind. It was useless to look down, for he could see only the top sides of the branches, so he stared upward and saw, far away in the blue, Rann, the Kite, balancing and wheeling as he kept watch over the jungle waiting for things to die. Rann noticed that the monkeys were carrying something, and dropped a few hundred yards to find out whether their load was good to eat. He whistled with surprise when he saw Mowgli being dragged up to a tree-top, and heard him give the Kite call for 'We be of one blood, thou and I.' The waves of the branches closed over the boy, but Rann balanced away to the next tree in time to see the little brown face come up again. 'Mark my trail!' Mowgli shouted. 'Tell Baloo of the Seeonee Pack, and Bagheera of the Council Rock.'

'In whose name, Brother?' Rann had never seen Mowgli before, though of course he had heard of him.

'Mowgli, the Frog. Man-cub they call me! Mark my tra—il!'

The last words were shrieked as he was being swung through the air, but Rann nodded, and rose up till he looked no bigger than a speck of dust, and there he hung, watching with his telescope eyes the swaying of the tree-tops as Mowgli's escort whirled along.

'They never go far,' he said, with a chuckle. 'They never do what they set out to do. Always pecking at new things are the Bandar-log. This time, if I have any eyesight, they have pecked down trouble for themselves, for Baloo is no fledgling and Bagheera can, as I know, kill more than goats.'

Then he rocked on his wings, his feet gathered up under him, and waited.

Meanwhile, Baloo and Bagheera were furious with rage and grief. Bagheera climbed as he had never climbed before, but the branches broke beneath his weight, and he slipped down, his claws full of bark.

'Why didst thou not warn the man-cub!' he roared to poor Baloo, who had set off at a clumsy trot in the hope of overtaking the monkeys. 'What was the use of half slaying him with blows if thou didst not warn him?'

'Haste! O haste! We—we may catch them yet!' Baloo panted.

'At that speed! It would not tire a wounded cow. Teacher of the Law, cub-beater—a mile of that rolling to and fro would burst thee open. Sit still and think! Make a plan. This is no time for chasing. They may drop him if we follow too close.'

'*Arrula! Whoo!* They may have dropped him already, being tired of carrying him. Who can trust the Bandar-log? Put dead bats on my head! Give me black bones to eat! Roll me into the hives of the wild bees that I may be stung to death, and bury me with the hyena; for I am the most miserable of bears! *Arulala! Wahooa!* O Mowgli, Mowgli! Why did I not warn thee against the Monkey Folk instead of breaking thy head? Now perhaps I may have knocked the day's lesson out of his mind, and he will be alone in the jungle without the Master Words!'

Baloo clasped his paws over his ears and rolled to and fro, moaning.

'At least he gave me all the Words correctly a little time ago,' said Bagheera, impatiently. 'Baloo, thou hast neither memory nor respect. What would the jungle think if I, the Black Panther, curled myself up like Ikki, the Porcupine, and howled?'

'What do I care what the jungle thinks? He may be dead by now.'

'Unless and until they drop him from the branches in sport, or kill him out of idleness, I have no fear for the man-cub. He is wise and well-taught, and, above all, he has the eyes that make the Jungle People afraid. But (and it is a great evil) he is in the power of the Bandar-log, and they, because they live in trees, have no fear of any of our people.' Bagheera licked his one fore paw thoughtfully.

'Fool that I am! Oh fat, brown, root-digging fool that I am!' said Baloo, uncoiling himself with a jerk. 'It is true what Hathi, the Wild Elephant, says: '*To each his own fear*'; and they, the Bandar-log, fear Kaa, the Rock Snake. He can climb as well as they can. He steals the young monkeys in the night. The mere whisper of his name makes their wicked tails cold. Let us go to Kaa.'

'What will he do for us? He is not of our tribe, being footless and with most evil eyes,' said Bagheera.

'He is very old and very cunning. Above all, he is always hungry,' said Baloo, hopefully. 'Promise him many goats.'

'He sleeps for a full month after he has once eaten. He may be asleep now, and even were he awake, what if he would rather kill his own goats?' Bagheera, who did not know much about Kaa, was naturally suspicious.

'Then in that case, thou and I together, old hunter, may make him see reason.' Here Baloo rubbed his faded brown shoulder against the panther, and they went off to look for Kaa, the Rock Python.

They found him stretched out on a warm ledge in the afternoon sun, admiring his beautiful new coat, for he had been in retirement for the last ten days changing his skin, and now he was very splendid—darting his big blunt-nosed head along the ground, and twisting the thirty feet of his body into fantastic knots and curves, and licking his lips as he thought of his dinner to come.

'He has not eaten,' said Baloo, with a grunt of relief, as soon as he saw the beautifully mottled brown and yellow jacket. 'Be careful, Bagheera! He is always a little blind after he has changed his skin, and very quick to strike.'

Kaa was not a poison snake—in fact he rather despised the Poison Snakes for cowards; but his strength lay in his hug, and when he had once lapped his huge coils round anybody there was no more to be said. 'Good hunting!' cried Baloo, sitting up on his haunches. Like all snakes of his breed Kaa was rather deaf, and did not hear the call at first. Then he curled up ready for any accident, his head lowered.

'Good hunting for us all,' he answered. 'Oho, Baloo, what dost thou do here? Good hunting, Bagheera. One of us at least needs food. Is there any news of game afoot? A doe now, or even a young buck? I am as empty as a dried well.'

'We are hunting,' said Baloo, carelessly. He knew that you must not hurry Kaa. He is too big.

'Give me permission to come with you,' said Kaa. 'A blow more or less is nothing to thee, Bagheera or Baloo, but I—I have to wait and wait for days in a wood path and climb half a night on the mere chance of a young ape. *Pss naw!* The branches are not what they were when I was young. Rotten twigs and dry boughs are they all.'

'Maybe thy great weight has something to do with the matter,' said Baloo.

'I am a fair length—a fair length,' said Kaa, with a little pride. 'But for all that, it is the fault of this new-grown timber.

I came very near to falling on my last hunt—very near indeed—and the noise of my slipping, for my tail was not tight wrapped round the tree, waked the Bandar-log, and they called me most evil names.'

'Footless, yellow earthworm,' said Bagheera under his whiskers, as though he were trying to remember something.

'*Sssss!* Have they ever called me *that*?' said Kaa.

'Something of that kind it was that they shouted to us last moon, but we never noticed them. They will say anything—even that thou hast lost all thy teeth, and dare not face anything bigger than a kid, because (they are indeed shameless, these Bandar-log)—because thou art afraid of the he-goats' horns,' Bagheera went on sweetly.

Now a snake, especially a wary old python like Kaa, very seldom shows that he is angry; but Baloo and Bagheera could see the big swallowing muscles on either side of Kaa's throat ripple and bulge.

'The Bandar-log have shifted their grounds,' he said, quietly. 'When I came up into the sun today I heard them whooping among the tree-tops.'

'It—it is the Bandar-log that we follow now,' said Baloo; but the words stuck in his throat, for this was the first time in his memory that one of the Jungle People had owned to being interested in the doings of the monkeys.

'Beyond doubt, then, it is no small thing that takes two such hunters—leaders in their own jungle, I am certain—on the trail of the Bandar-log,' Kaa replied, courteously, as he swelled with curiosity.

'Indeed,' Baloo began, 'I am no more than the old, and sometimes very foolish, Teacher of the Law to the Seeonee wolf-cubs, and Bagheera here—'

'Is Bagheera,' said the Black Panther, and his jaws shut with a snap, for he did not believe in being humble. 'The trouble is this, Kaa. Those nut-stealers and pickers of palm-leaves have stolen away our man-cub, of whom thou hast perhaps heard.'

'I heard some news from Ikki (his quills make him presumptuous) of a man-thing that was entered into a wolf-pack, but I did not believe. Ikki is full of stories half heard and very badly told.'

'But it is true. He is such a man-cub as never was,' said Baloo. 'The best and wisest and boldest of man-cubs. My own pupil, who shall make the name of Baloo famous through all the jungles; and besides, I—we—love him, Kaa.'

'*Ts! Ts!*' said Kaa, shaking his head to and fro. 'I also have known what love is. There are tales I could tell that—'

'That need a clear night when we are all well fed to praise properly,' said Bagheera, quickly. 'Our man-cub is in the hands of the Bandar-log now, and we know that of all the Jungle People they fear Kaa alone.'

'They fear me alone. They have good reason,' said Kaa. 'Chattering, foolish, vain—vain, foolish, and chattering—are the monkeys. But a man-thing in their hands is in no good luck. They grow tired of the nuts they pick, and throw them down. They carry a branch half a day, meaning to do great things with it, and then they snap it in two. That manling is not to be envied. They called me also—'yellow fish,' was it not?'

'Worm—worm—earthworm,' said Bagheera; 'as well as other things which I cannot now say for shame.'

'We must remind them to speak well of their master. *Aaa-sssh!* We must help their wandering memories. Now, whither went they with thy cub?'

'The jungle alone knows. Towards the sunset, I believe,'

said Baloo. 'We had thought that thou wouldst know, Kaa.'

'I? How? I take them when they come in my way, but I do not hunt the Bandar-log—or frogs—or green scum on a water-hole, for that matter.'

'Up, up! Up, up! *Hillo! Illo! Illo!* Look up, Baloo of the Seeonee Wolf Pack!'

Baloo looked up to see where the voice came from, and there was Rann, the Kite, sweeping down with the sun shining on the upturned flanges of his wings. It was near Rann's bedtime, but he had ranged all over the jungle looking for the bear, and missed him in the thick foliage.

'What is it?' said Baloo.

'I have seen Mowgli among the Bandar-log. He bade me tell you. I watched. The Bandar-log have taken him beyond the river to the Monkey City—to the Cold Lairs. They may stay there for a night, or ten nights, or an hour. I have told the bats to watch through the dark time. That is my message. Good hunting, all you below!'

'Full gorge and a deep sleep to you, Rann!' cried Bagheera. 'I will remember thee in my next kill, and put aside the head for thee alone, O best of kites!'

'It is nothing. It is nothing. The boy held the Master Word. I could have done no less,' and Rann circled up again to his roost.

'He has not forgotten to use his tongue,' said Baloo, with a chuckle of pride. 'To think of one so young remembering the Master Word for the birds while he was being pulled across trees!'

'It was most firmly driven into him,' said Bagheera. 'But I am proud of him, and now we must go to the Cold Lairs.'

They all knew where that place was, but few of the Jungle People ever went there, because what they called the Cold Lairs was an old deserted city, lost and buried in the jungle, and beasts seldom use a place that men have once used. The wild boar will, but the hunting-tribes do not. Besides, the monkeys lived there as much as they could be said to live anywhere, and no self-respecting animal would come within eye-shot of it except in times of drouth, when the half-ruined tanks and reservoirs held a little water.

'It is half a night's journey—at full speed,' said Bagheera. Baloo looked very serious. 'I will go as fast as I can,' he said, anxiously.

'We dare not wait for thee. Follow, Baloo. We must go on the quick-foot—Kaa and I.'

'Feet or no feet, I can keep abreast of all thy four,' said Kaa, shortly.

Baloo made one effort to hurry, but had to sit down panting, and so they left him to come on later, while Bagheera hurried forward, at the rocking panther-canter. Kaa said nothing, but, strive as Bagheera might, the huge Rock Python held level with him. When they came to a hill-stream, Bagheera gained, because he bounded across while Kaa swam, his head and two feet of his neck clearing the water, but on level ground Kaa made up the distance.

'By the Broken Lock that freed me,' said Bagheera, when twilight had fallen, 'thou art no slow-goer.'

'I am hungry,' said Kaa. 'Besides, they called me speckled frog.'

'Worm—earthworm, and yellow to boot.'

'All one. Let us go on,' and Kaa seemed to pour himself along the ground, finding the shortest road with his steady eyes, and keeping to it.

In the Cold Lairs the Monkey People were not thinking of Mowgli's friends at all. They had brought the boy to the Lost

City, and were very pleased with themselves for the time. Mowgli had never seen an Indian city before, and though this was almost a heap of ruins it seemed very wonderful and splendid. Some king had built it long ago on a little hill. You could still trace the stone causeways that led up to the ruined gates where the last splinters of wood hung to the worn, rusted hinges. Trees had grown into and out of the walls; the battlements were tumbled down and decayed, and wild creepers hung out of the windows of the towers on the walls in bushy hanging clumps.

A great roofless palace crowned the hill, and the marble of the courtyards and the fountains was split and stained with red and green, and the very cobblestones in the courtyard where the king's elephants used to live had been thrust up and apart by grasses and young trees. From the palace you could see the rows and rows of roofless houses that made up the city, looking like empty honeycombs filled with blackness; the shapeless block of stone that had been an idol in the square where four roads met; the pits and dimples at street corners where the public wells once stood, and the shattered domes of temples with wild figs sprouting on their sides.

The monkeys called the place their city, and pretended to despise the Jungle People because they lived in the forest. And yet they never knew what the buildings were made for nor how to use them. They would sit in circles on the hall of the king's council-chamber, and scratch for fleas and pretend to be men; or they would run in and out of the roofless houses and collect pieces of plaster and old bricks in a corner, and forget where they had hidden them, and fight and cry in scuffling crowds, and then break off to play up and down the terraces of the king's garden, where they would shake the rose-trees and the oranges in sport to see the fruit and flowers fall. They explored all the passages and dark tunnels in the palace and the hundreds of little dark rooms; but they never remembered what they had seen and what they had not, and so drifted about in ones and twos or crowds, telling one another that they were doing as men did. They drank at the tanks and made the water all muddy, and then they fought over it, and then they would all rush together in mobs and shout: 'There are none in the jungle so wise and good and clever and strong and gentle as the Bandar-log.' Then all would begin again till they grew tired of the city and went back to the tree-tops, hoping the Jungle People would notice them.

Mowgli, who had been trained under the Law of the Jungle, did not like or understand this kind of life. The monkeys dragged him into the Cold Lairs late in the afternoon, and instead of going to sleep, as Mowgli would have done after a long journey, they joined hands and danced about and sang their foolish songs.

One of the monkeys made a speech, and told his companions that Mowgli's capture marked a new thing in the history of the Bandar-log, for Mowgli was going to show them how to weave sticks and canes together as a protection against rain and cold. Mowgli picked up some creepers and began to work them in and out, and the monkeys tried to imitate; but in a very few minutes they lost interest and began to pull their friends' tails or jump up and down on all fours, coughing.

'I want to eat,' said Mowgli. 'I am a stranger in this part of the jungle. Bring me food, or give me leave to hunt here.'

Twenty or thirty monkeys bounded away to bring him nuts and wild pawpaws; but they fell to fighting on the road, and it was too much trouble to go back with what was left of the fruit. Mowgli was sore and angry as well as hungry, and he roamed through the empty city giving the Strangers' Hunting

Call from time to time, but no one answered him, and Mowgli felt that he had reached a very bad place indeed.

'All that Baloo has said about the Bandar-log is true,' he thought to himself. 'They have no Law, no Hunting Call, and no leaders—nothing but foolish words and little picking, thievish hands. So if I am starved or killed here, it will be all my own fault. But I must try to return to my own jungle. Baloo will surely beat me, but that is better than chasing silly rose-leaves with the Bandar-log.'

But no sooner had he walked to the city wall than the monkeys pulled him back, telling him that he did not know how happy he was, and pinching him to make him grateful. He set his teeth and said nothing, but went with the shouting monkeys to a terrace above the red sandstone reservoirs that were half full of rainwater. There was a ruined summer-house of white marble in the center of the terrace, built for queens dead a hundred years ago. The domed roof had half fallen in and blocked up the underground passage from the palace by which the queens used to enter; but the walls were made of screens of marble tracery—beautiful, milk-white fretwork, set with agates and cornelians and jasper and lapis lazuli, and as the moon came up behind the hill it shone through the openwork, casting shadows on the ground like black-velvet embroidery.

Sore, sleepy, and hungry as he was, Mowgli could not help laughing when the Bandar-log began, twenty at a time, to tell him how great and wise and strong and gentle they were, and how foolish he was to wish to leave them. 'We are great. We are free. We are wonderful. We are the most wonderful people in all the jungle! We all say so, and so it must be true,' they shouted. 'Now as you are a new listener and can carry our words back to the Jungle People so that they may notice us in future, we will tell you all about our most excellent selves.'

Mowgli made no objection, and the monkeys gathered by hundreds and hundreds on the terrace to listen to their own speakers singing the praises of the Bandar-log, and whenever a speaker stopped for want of breath they would all shout together: 'This is true; we all say so.'

Mowgli nodded and blinked, and said 'Yes' when they asked him a question, and his head spun with the noise. 'Tabaqui, the Jackal, must have bitten all these people,' he said to himself, 'and now they have the madness. Certainly this is *dewance*—the madness. Do they never go to sleep? Now there is a cloud coming to cover that moon. If it were only a big enough cloud I might try to run away in the darkness. But I am tired.'

That same cloud was being watched by two good friends in the ruined ditch below the city wall, for Bagheera and Kaa, knowing well how dangerous the Monkey People were in large numbers, did not wish to run any risks. The monkeys never fight unless they are a hundred to one, and few in the jungle care for those odds.

'I will go to the west wall,' Kaa whispered, 'and come down swiftly with the slope of the ground in my favour. They will not throw themselves upon *my* back in their hundreds, but—'

'I know it,' said Bagheera. 'Would that Baloo were here; but we must do what we can. When that cloud covers the moon I shall go to the terrace. They hold some sort of council there over the boy.'

'Good hunting,' said Kaa, grimly, and glided away to the west wall. That happened to be the least ruined of any, and the big snake was delayed a while before he could find a way up the stones.

The cloud hid the moon, and as Mowgli wondered what

would come next he heard Bagheera's light feet on the terrace. The Black Panther had raced up the slope almost without a sound, and was striking—he knew better than to waste time in biting—right and left among the monkeys, who were seated round Mowgli in circles fifty and sixty deep. There was a howl of fright and rage, and then as Bagheera tripped on the rolling, kicking bodies beneath him, a monkey shouted: 'There is only one here! Kill him! Kill!' A scuffling mass of monkeys, biting, scratching, tearing, and pulling, closed over Bagheera, while five or six laid hold of Mowgli, dragged him up the wall of the summer-house, and pushed him through the hole of the broken dome. A man-trained boy would have been badly bruised, for the fall was a good ten feet, but Mowgli fell as Baloo had taught him to fall, and landed light.

'Stay there,' shouted the monkeys, 'till we have killed thy friend. Later we will play with thee, if the Poison People leave thee alive.'

'We be of one blood, ye and I,' said Mowgli, quickly giving the Snake's Call. He could hear rustling and hissing in the rubbish all round him, and gave the Call a second time to make sure.

'Down hoods all,' said half a dozen low voices. Every old ruin in India becomes sooner or later a dwelling-place of snakes, and the old summer-house was alive with cobras. 'Stand still, Little Brother, lest thy feet do us harm.'

Mowgli stood as quietly as he could, peering through the openwork and listening to the furious din of the fight round the Black Panther—the yells and chatterings and scufflings, and Bagheera's deep, hoarse cough as he backed and bucked and twisted and plunged under the heaps of his enemies. For the first time since he was born, Bagheera was fighting for his life.

'Baloo must be at hand; Bagheera would not have come

alone,' Mowgli thought; and then he called aloud: 'To the tank, Bagheera! Roll to the water-tanks! Roll and plunge! Get to the water!'

Bagheera heard, and the cry that told him Mowgli was safe gave him new courage. He worked his way desperately, inch by inch, straight for the reservoirs, hitting in silence.

Then from the ruined wall nearest the jungle rose up the rumbling war-shout of Baloo. The old bear had done his best, but he could not come before. 'Bagheera,' he shouted, 'I am here! I climb! I haste! *Ahuwora!* The stones slip under my feet! Wait my coming, O most infamous Bandar-log!'

He panted up the terrace only to disappear to the head in a wave of monkeys, but he threw himself squarely on his haunches, and spreading out his fore paws, hugged as many as he could hold, and then began to hit with a regular *bat-bat-bat*, like the flipping strokes of a paddle-wheel.

A crash and a splash told Mowgli that Bagheera had fought his way to the tank, where the monkeys could not follow. The panther lay gasping for breath, his head just out of water, while the monkeys stood three deep on the red stone steps, dancing up and down with rage, ready to spring upon him from all sides if he came out to help Baloo. It was then that Bagheera lifted up his dripping chin, and in despair gave the Snake's Call for protection—'We be of one blood, ye and I'—for he believed that Kaa had turned tail at the last minute. Even Baloo, half smothered under the monkeys on the edge of the terrace, could not help chuckling as he heard the big Black Panther asking for help.

Kaa had only just worked his way over the west wall, landing with a wrench that dislodged a coping-stone into the ditch. He had no intention of losing any advantage of the ground, and coiled and uncoiled himself once or twice, to be sure that every foot of his long body was in working order.

All that while the fight with Baloo went on, and the monkeys yelled in the tank round Bagheera, and Mang, the Bat, flying to and fro, carried the news of the great battle over the jungle, till even Hathi, the Wild Elephant, trumpeted, and, far away, scattered bands of the Monkey Folk woke and came leaping along the tree-roads to help their comrades in the Cold Lairs, and the noise of the fight roused all the day-birds for miles round.

Then Kaa came straight, quickly, and anxious to kill. The fighting strength of a python is in the driving blow of his head, backed by all the strength and weight of his body. If you can imagine a lance, or a battering-ram, or a hammer, weighing nearly half a ton driven by a cool, quiet mind living in the handle of it, you can imagine roughly what Kaa was like when he fought. A python four or five feet long can knock a man down if he hits him fairly in the chest, and Kaa was thirty feet long, as you know. His first stroke was delivered into the heart of the crowd round Baloo—sent home with shut mouth in silence—and there was no need of a second. The monkeys scattered with cries of 'Kaa! It is Kaa! Run! Run!'

Generations of monkeys had been scared into good behaviour by the stories their elders told them of Kaa, the night-thief, who could slip along the branches as quietly as moss grows, and steal away the strongest monkey that ever lived; of old Kaa, who could make himself look so like a dead branch or a rotten stump that the wisest were deceived till the branch caught them, and then—

Kaa was everything that the monkeys feared in the jungle, for none of them knew the limits of his power, none of them could look him in the face, and none had ever come alive out of his hug. And so they ran, stammering with terror, to the walls and the roofs of the houses, and Baloo drew a deep breath of relief. His fur was much thicker than Bagheera's, but he had suffered sorely in the fight. Then Kaa opened his mouth for the first time and spoke one long hissing word, and the far-away monkeys, hurrying to the defense of the Cold Lairs, stayed where they were, cowering, till the loaded branches bent and crackled under them. The monkeys on the walls and the empty houses stopped their cries, and in the stillness that fell upon the city Mowgli heard Bagheera shaking his wet sides as he came up from the tank.

Then the clamour broke out again. The monkeys leaped higher up the walls; they clung round the necks of the big stone idols and shrieked as they skipped along the battlements; while Mowgli, dancing in the summer-house, put his eye to the screenwork and hooted owl-fashion between his front teeth, to show his derision and contempt.

'Get the man-cub out of that trap; I can do no more,' Bagheera gasped. 'Let us take the man-cub and go. They may attack again.'

'They will not move till I order them. Stay you sssso!' Kaa hissed, and the city was silent once more. 'I could not come before, Brother, but I *think* I heard thee call'—this was to Bagheera.

'I—I may have cried out in the battle,' Bagheera answered. 'Baloo, art thou hurt?'

'I am not sure that they have not pulled me into a hundred little bearlings,' said Baloo, gravely shaking one leg after the other. 'Wow! I am sore. Kaa, we owe thee, I think, our lives—Bagheera and I.'

'No matter. Where is the manling?'

'Here, in a trap. I cannot climb out,' cried Mowgli. The curve of the broken dome was above his head.

'Take him away. He dances like Mao, the Peacock. He will crush our young,' said the cobras inside.

'Hah!' said Kaa, with a chuckle, 'he has friends everywhere, this manling. Stand back, Manling; and hide you, O Poison People. I break down the wall.'

Kaa looked carefully till he found a discolored crack in the marble tracery showing a weak spot, made two or three light taps with his head to get the distance, and then lifting up six feet of his body clear of the ground, sent home half a dozen full-power, smashing blows, nose-first. The screenwork broke and fell away in a cloud of dust and rubbish, and Mowgli leaped through the opening and flung himself between Baloo and Bagheera—an arm round each big neck.

'Art thou hurt?' said Baloo, hugging him softly.

'I am sore, hungry, and not a little bruised; but, oh, they have handled ye grievously, my Brothers! Ye bleed.'

'Others also,' said Bagheera, licking his lips and looking at the monkey-dead on the terrace and round the tank.

'It is nothing, it is nothing if thou art safe, O my pride of all little frogs!' whimpered Baloo.

'Of that we shall judge later,' said Bagheera, in a dry voice that Mowgli did not at all like. 'But here is Kaa, to whom we owe the battle and thou owest thy life. Thank him according to our customs, Mowgli.'

Mowgli turned and saw the great python's head swaying a foot above his own.

'So this is the manling,' said Kaa. 'Very soft is his skin, and he is not so unlike the Bandar-log. Have a care, Manling, that I do not mistake thee for a monkey some twilight when

I have newly changed my coat.'

'We be of one blood, thou and I,' Mowgli answered. 'I take my life from thee, tonight. My kill shall be thy kill if ever thou art hungry, O Kaa.'

'All thanks, Little Brother,' said Kaa, though his eyes twinkled. 'And what may so bold a hunter kill? I ask that I may follow when next he goes abroad.'

'I kill nothing—I am too little—but I drive goats towards such as can use them. When thou art empty come to me and see if I speak the truth. I have some skill in these [he held out his hands], and if ever thou art in a trap, I may pay the debt which I owe to thee, to Bagheera, and to Baloo, here. Good hunting to ye all, my masters.'

'Well said,' growled Baloo, for Mowgli had returned thanks very prettily. The python dropped his head lightly for a minute on Mowgli's shoulder. 'A brave heart and a courteous tongue,' said he. 'They shall carry thee far through the jungle, Manling. But now go hence quickly with thy friends. Go and sleep, for the moon sets, and what follows it is not well that thou shouldst see.'

The moon was sinking behind the hills and the lines of trembling monkeys huddled together on the walls and battlements looked like ragged, shaky fringes of things. Baloo went down to the tank for a drink, and Bagheera began to put his fur in order, as Kaa glided out into the centre of the terrace and brought his jaws together with a ringing snap that drew all the monkeys' eyes upon him.

'The moon sets,' he said. 'Is there yet light to see?'

From the walls came a moan like the wind in the tree-tops: 'We see, O Kaa!'

'Good! Begins now the Dance—the Dance of the Hunger

of Kaa. Sit still and watch.'

He turned twice or thrice in a big circle, weaving his head from right to left. Then he began making loops and figures of eight with his body, and soft, oozy triangles that melted into squares and five-sided figures, and coiled mounds, never resting, never hurrying, and never stopping his low, humming song. It grew darker and darker, till at last the dragging, shifting coils disappeared, but they could hear the rustle of the scales.

Baloo and Bagheera stood still as stone, growling in their throats, their neck-hair bristling, and Mowgli watched and wondered.

'Bandar-log,' said the voice of Kaa at last, 'can ye stir foot or hand without my order? Speak!'

'Without thy order we cannot stir foot or hand, O Kaa!'

'Good! Come all one pace nearer to me.'

The lines of the monkeys swayed forward helplessly, and Baloo and Bagheera took one stiff step forward with them.

'Nearer!' hissed Kaa, and they all moved again.

Mowgli laid his hands on Baloo and Bagheera to get them away, and the two great beasts started as though they had been waked from a dream.

'Keep thy hand on my shoulder,' Bagheera whispered. 'Keep it there, or I must go back—must go back to Kaa. *Aah!*'

'It is only old Kaa making circles on the dust,' said Mowgli; 'let us go'; and the three slipped off through a gap in the walls to the jungle.

'*Whoof!*' said Baloo, when he stood under the still trees again. 'Never more will I make an ally of Kaa,' and he shook himself all over.

'He knows more than we,' said Bagheera, trembling. 'In a little time, had I stayed, I should have walked down his throat.'

'Many will walk that road before the moon rises again,' said Baloo. 'He will have good hunting—after his own fashion.'

'But what was the meaning of it all?' said Mowgli, who did not know anything of a python's powers of fascination. 'I saw no more than a big snake making foolish circles till the dark came. And his nose was all sore. Ho! Ho!'

'Mowgli,' said Bagheera, angrily, 'his nose was sore on *thy* account; as my ears and sides and paws, and Baloo's neck and shoulders are bitten on *thy* account. Neither Baloo nor Bagheera will be able to hunt with pleasure for many days.'

'It is nothing,' said Baloo; 'we have the man-cub again.'

'True; but he has cost us most heavily in time which might have been spent in good hunting, in wounds, in hair—I am half plucked along my back—and last of all, in honour. For, remember, Mowgli, I, who am the Black Panther, was forced to call upon Kaa for protection, and Baloo and I were both made stupid as little birds by the Hunger-Dance. All this, Man-cub, came of thy playing with the Bandar-log.'

'True; it is true,' said Mowgli, sorrowfully. 'I am an evil man-cub, and my stomach is sad in me.'

'*Mf!* What says the Law of the Jungle, Baloo?'

Baloo did not wish to bring Mowgli into any more trouble, but he could not tamper with the Law, so he mumbled, 'Sorrow never stays punishment. But remember, Bagheera, he is very little.'

'I will remember; but he has done mischief; and blows must be dealt now. Mowgli, hast thou anything to say?'

'Nothing. I did wrong. Baloo and thou art wounded. It is just.'

Bagheera gave him half a dozen love-taps; from a panther's point of view they would hardly have waked one of his own cubs, but for a seven year-old boy they amounted to as severe a beating as you could wish to avoid. When it was all over Mowgli sneezed, and picked himself up without a word.

'Now,' said Bagheera, 'jump on my back, Little Brother, and we will go home.'

One of the beauties of Jungle Law is that punishment settles all scores. There is no nagging afterward.

Mowgli laid his head down on Bagheera's back and slept so deeply that he never waked when he was put down by Mother Wolf's side in the home-cave.

Mr Badger

KENNETH GRAHAME

They waited patiently for what seemed a very long time, stamping in the snow to keep their feet warm. At last they heard the sound of slow shuffling footsteps approaching the door from the inside. It seemed, as the Mole remarked to the Rat, like some one walking in carpet slippers that were too large for him and down at heel; which was intelligent of Mole, because that was exactly what it was.

There was the noise of a bolt shot back, and the door opened a few inches, enough to show a long snout and a pair of sleepy blinking eyes.

'Now, the VERY next time this happens,' said a gruff and suspicious voice, 'I shall be exceedingly angry. Who is it this time, disturbing people on such a night? Speak up!'

'Oh, Badger,' cried the Rat, 'let us in, please. It's me, Rat, and my friend Mole, and we've lost our way in the snow.'

'What, Ratty, my dear little man!' exclaimed the Badger, in quite a different voice. 'Come along in, both of you, at once. Why, you must be perished. Well I never! Lost in the snow! And in the Wild Wood, too, and at this time of night! But come in with you.'

The two animals tumbled over each other in their eagerness to get inside, and heard the door shut behind them with great joy and relief.

The Badger, who wore a long dressing-gown, and whose slippers were indeed very down at heel, carried a flat candlestick in his paw and had probably been on his way to bed when their summons sounded. He looked kindly down on them and patted both their heads. 'This is not the sort of night for small animals to be out,' he said paternally. 'I'm afraid you've been up to some of your pranks again, Ratty. But come along; come into the kitchen. There's a first-rate fire there, and supper and everything.'

He shuffled on in front of them, carrying the light, and they followed him, nudging each other in an anticipating sort of way, down a long, gloomy, and, to tell the truth, decidedly shabby passage, into a sort of a central hall; out of which they could dimly see other long tunnel-like passages branching, passages mysterious and without apparent end. But there were doors in the hall as well—stout oaken comfortable-looking doors. One of these the Badger flung open, and at once they found themselves in all the glow and warmth of a large fire-lit kitchen.

The floor was well-worn red brick, and on the wide hearth burnt a fire of logs, between two attractive chimney-corners tucked away in the wall, well out of any suspicion of draught. A couple of high-backed settles, facing each other on either side of the fire, gave further sitting accommodations for the sociably disposed. In the middle of the room stood a long table of plain boards placed on trestles, with benches down each side. At one end of it, where an arm-chair stood pushed back, were spread the remains of the Badger's plain but ample supper. Rows of spotless plates winked from the shelves of the dresser at the far end of the room, and from the rafters overhead hung hams, bundles of dried herbs, nets of onions, and baskets of eggs. It seemed a place where heroes could fitly feast after victory, where weary harvesters could line up in scores along the table and keep their Harvest Home with mirth and song, or where two or three friends of simple tastes could sit about as they pleased and eat and smoke and talk in comfort and contentment. The ruddy brick floor smiled up at the smoky ceiling; the oaken settles, shiny with long wear, exchanged cheerful glances with each other; plates on the dresser grinned at pots on the shelf, and the merry firelight flickered and played over everything without distinction.

The kindly Badger thrust them down on a settle to toast themselves at the fire, and bade them remove their wet coats and boots. Then he fetched them dressing-gowns and slippers, and himself bathed the Mole's shin with warm water and mended the cut with sticking-plaster till the whole thing was just as good as new, if not better. In the embracing light and warmth, warm and dry at last, with weary legs propped up in front of them, and a suggestive clink of plates being arranged on the table behind, it seemed to the storm-driven animals, now in safe anchorage, that the cold and trackless Wild Wood just left outside was miles and miles away, and all that they had suffered in it a half-forgotten dream.

When at last they were thoroughly toasted, the Badger summoned them to the table, where he had been busy laying a repast. They had felt pretty hungry before, but when they actually saw at last the supper that was spread for them, really it seemed only a question of what they should attack first where all was so attractive, and whether the other things would obligingly wait for them till they had time to give them attention. Conversation was impossible for a long time; and when it was slowly resumed, it was that regrettable sort of conversation that results from talking with your mouth full. The Badger did not mind that sort of thing at all, nor did he take any notice of elbows on the table, or everybody speaking at once. As he did not go into Society himself, he had got an idea that these things belonged to the things that didn't really matter. (We know of course that he was wrong, and took too narrow a view; because they do matter very much, though it would take too long to explain why.) He sat in his arm-chair at the head of the table, and nodded gravely at intervals as the animals told their story; and he did not seem surprised or shocked at anything, and he never said, 'I told you so,' or, 'Just what I always said,' or remarked that they ought to have done so-and-so, or ought not to have done something else. The Mole began to feel very friendly towards him.

When supper was really finished at last, and each animal felt that his skin was now as tight as was decently safe, and that by this time he didn't care a hang for anybody or anything, they gathered round the glowing embers of the great wood fire, and thought how jolly it was to be sitting up SO late, and SO independent, and SO full; and after they had chatted for a time about things in general, the Badger said heartily, 'Now then! tell us the news from your part of the world. How's old Toad going on?'

'Oh, from bad to worse,' said the Rat gravely, while the Mole, cocked up on a settle and basking in the firelight, his heels higher than his head, tried to look properly mournful. 'Another smash-up only last week, and a bad one. You see, he will insist on driving himself, and he's hopelessly incapable. If he'd only employ a decent, steady, well-trained animal, pay him good wages, and leave everything to him, he'd get on all right. But no; he's convinced he's a heaven-born driver, and nobody can teach him anything; and all the rest follows.'

'How many has he had?' inquired the Badger gloomily.

'Smashes, or machines?' asked the Rat. 'Oh, well, after all, it's the same thing—with Toad. This is the seventh. As for the others—you know that coach-house of his? Well, it's piled up—literally piled up to the roof—with fragments of motor-cars, none of them bigger than your hat! That accounts for the other six—so far as they can be accounted for.'

'He's been in hospital three times,' put in the Mole; 'and as for the fines he's had to pay, it's simply awful to think of.'

'Yes, and that's part of the trouble,' continued the Rat. 'Toad's rich, we all know; but he's not a millionaire. And he's a hopelessly bad driver, and quite regardless of law and order. Killed or ruined—it's got to be one of the two things, sooner or later. Badger! We're his friends—oughtn't we to do something?'

The Badger went through a bit of hard thinking. 'Now look here!' he said at last, rather severely; 'of course you know I can't do anything NOW?'

His two friends assented, quite understanding his point. No animal, according to the rules of animal-etiquette, is ever expected to do anything strenuous, or heroic, or even moderately active during the off-season of winter. All are sleepy—some actually asleep. All are weather-bound, more or less; and all are resting from arduous days and nights, during which every muscle in them has been severely tested, and every energy kept at full stretch.

'Very well then!' continued the Badger. 'BUT, when once the year has really turned, and the nights are shorter, and halfway through them one rouses and feels fidgety and wanting to be up and doing by sunrise, if not before—YOU know!—'

Both animals nodded gravely. THEY knew!

'Well, THEN,' went on the Badger, 'we—that is, you and me and our friend the Mole here—we'll take Toad seriously in hand. We'll stand no nonsense whatever. We'll bring him back to reason, by force if need be. We'll MAKE him be a sensible Toad. We'll—you're asleep, Rat!'

'Not me!' said the Rat, waking up with a jerk.

'He's been asleep two or three times since supper,' said the Mole, laughing. He himself was feeling quite wakeful and even lively, though he didn't know why. The reason was, of course, that he being naturally an underground animal by birth and breeding, the situation of Badger's house exactly suited him and made him feel at home; while the Rat, who slept every night in a bedroom the windows of which opened on a breezy river, naturally felt the atmosphere still and oppressive.

'Well, it's time we were all in bed,' said the Badger, getting up and fetching flat candlesticks. 'Come along, you two, and I'll show you your quarters. And take your time tomorrow morning—breakfast at any hour you please!'

He conducted the two animals to a long room that seemed half bedchamber and half loft. The Badger's winter stores, which indeed were visible everywhere, took up half the room—piles of apples, turnips, and potatoes, baskets full of nuts, and jars of honey; but the two little white beds on the remainder of the floor looked soft and inviting, and the linen on them, though coarse, was clean and smelt beautifully of lavender; and the Mole and the Water Rat, shaking off their garments in some thirty seconds, tumbled in between the sheets in great joy and contentment.

In accordance with the kindly Badger's injunctions, the two tired animals came down to breakfast very late next morning, and found a bright fire burning in the kitchen, and two young hedgehogs sitting on a bench at the table, eating oatmeal porridge out of wooden bowls. The hedgehogs dropped their spoons, rose to their feet, and ducked their heads respectfully as the two entered.

'There, sit down, sit down,' said the Rat pleasantly, 'and go on with your porridge. Where have you youngsters come from? Lost your way in the snow, I suppose?'

'Yes, please, sir,' said the elder of the two hedgehogs respectfully. 'Me and little Billy here, we was trying to find our way to school—mother WOULD have us go, was the weather ever so—and of course we lost ourselves, sir, and Billy he got frightened and took and cried, being young and faint-hearted. And at last we happened up against Mr Badger's back door, and made so bold as to knock, sir, for Mr Badger he's a kind-hearted gentleman, as everyone knows——'

'I understand,' said the Rat, cutting himself some rashers from a side of bacon, while the Mole dropped some eggs into a saucepan. 'And what's the weather like outside? You needn't 'sir' me quite so much?' he added.

'O, terrible bad, sir, terrible deep the snow is,' said the hedgehog. 'No getting out for the likes of you gentlemen to-day.'

'Where's Mr Badger?' inquired the Mole, as he warmed the coffee-pot before the fire.

'The master's gone into his study, sir,' replied the hedgehog, 'and he said as how he was going to be particular busy this morning, and on no account was he to be disturbed.'

This explanation, of course, was thoroughly understood by every one present. The fact is, as already set forth, when you live a life of intense activity for six months in the year, and of comparative or actual somnolence for the other six, during the latter period you cannot be continually pleading sleepiness when there are people about or things to be done. The excuse gets monotonous. The animals well knew that Badger, having eaten a hearty breakfast, had retired to his study and settled himself in an arm-chair with his legs up on another and a red cotton handkerchief over his face, and was being 'busy' in the usual way at this time of the year.

The front-door bell clanged loudly, and the Rat, who was very greasy with buttered toast, sent Billy, the smaller hedgehog, to see who it might be. There was a sound of much stamping in the hall, and presently Billy returned in front of the Otter, who threw himself on the Rat with an embrace and a shout of affectionate greeting.

'Get off!' spluttered the Rat, with his mouth full.

'Thought I should find you here all right,' said the Otter cheerfully. 'They were all in a great state of alarm along River Bank when I arrived this morning. Rat never been home all night—nor Mole either—something dreadful must have happened, they said; and the snow had covered up all your tracks, of course. But I knew that when people were in any fix they mostly went to Badger, or else Badger got to know of it somehow, so I came straight off here, through the Wild Wood and the snow! My! it was fine, coming through the snow as the red sun was rising and showing against the black tree-trunks! As you went along in the stillness, every now and then masses of snow slid off the branches suddenly with a flop! making you jump and run for cover. Snow-castles and snow-caverns had sprung up out of nowhere in the night—and snow bridges, terraces, ramparts—I could have stayed and played with them for hours. Here and there great branches had been torn away by the sheer weight of the snow, and robins perched and hopped on them in their perky conceited way, just as if they had done it themselves. A ragged string of wild geese passed overhead, high on the grey sky, and a few rooks whirled over the trees, inspected, and flapped off homewards with a disgusted expression; but I met no sensible being to ask the news of. About halfway across I came on a rabbit sitting on a stump, cleaning his silly face with his paws. He was a pretty scared animal when I crept up behind him and placed a heavy forepaw on his shoulder. I had to cuff his head once or twice to get any sense out of it at all. At last I managed to extract from him that Mole had been seen in the Wild Wood last night by one of them. It was the talk of the burrows, he said, how Mole, Mr Rat's particular friend, was in a bad fix; how he had lost his way, and 'They' were up and out hunting, and were chivvying him round and round. 'Then why didn't any of you DO something?' I asked. 'You mayn't be blest with brains, but there are hundreds and hundreds of you, big, stout fellows, as fat as butter, and your burrows running in all directions, and you could have taken him in and made him safe and comfortable, or tried to, at all events.' 'What, US?' he merely said: 'DO something? us rabbits?' So I cuffed him again and left him. There was nothing else to be done. At any rate, I had learnt something; and if I had had the luck to meet any of 'Them' I'd have learnt something more—or THEY would.'

'Weren't you at all—er—nervous?' asked the Mole, some of yesterday's terror coming back to him at the mention of the Wild Wood.

'Nervous?' The Otter showed a gleaming set of strong white teeth as he laughed. 'I'd give 'em nerves if any of them tried anything on with me. Here, Mole, fry me some slices of ham, like the good little chap you are. I'm frightfully hungry, and I've got any amount to say to Ratty here. Haven't seen him for an age.'

So the good-natured Mole, having cut some slices of ham, set the hedgehogs to fry it, and returned to his own breakfast, while the Otter and the Rat, their heads together, eagerly talked river-shop, which is long shop and talk that is endless, running on like the babbling river itself.

A plate of fried ham had just been cleared and sent back for more, when the Badger entered, yawning and rubbing his eyes, and greeted them all in his quiet, simple way, with kind enquiries for every one. 'It must be getting on for luncheon time,' he remarked to the Otter. 'Better stop and have it with us. You must be hungry, this cold morning.'

'Rather!' replied the Otter, winking at the Mole. 'The sight of these greedy young hedgehogs stuffing themselves with fried ham makes me feel positively famished.'

The hedgehogs, who were just beginning to feel hungry again after their porridge, and after working so hard at their frying, looked timidly up at Mr Badger, but were too shy to say anything.

'Here, you two youngsters be off home to your mother,' said the Badger kindly. 'I'll send some one with you to show you the way. You won't want any dinner to-day, I'll be bound.'

He gave them sixpence apiece and a pat on the head, and they went off with much respectful swinging of caps and touching of forelocks.

Presently they all sat down to luncheon together. The Mole found himself placed next to Mr Badger, and, as the other two were still deep in river-gossip from which nothing could divert them, he took the opportunity to tell Badger how comfortable and home-like it all felt to him. 'Once well underground,' he said, 'you know exactly where you are. Nothing can happen to you, and nothing can get at you. You're entirely your own master, and you don't have to consult anybody or mind what they say. Things go on all the same overhead, and you let 'em, and don't bother about 'em. When you want to, up you go, and there the things are, waiting for you.'

The Badger simply beamed on him. 'That's exactly what I say,' he replied. 'There's no security, or peace and tranquillity, except underground. And then, if your ideas get larger and you want to expand—why, a dig and a scrape, and there you are! If you feel your house is a bit too big, you stop up a hole or two, and there you are again! No builders, no tradesmen, no remarks passed on you by fellows looking over your wall, and, above all, no WEATHER. Look at Rat, now. A couple of feet of flood water, and he's got to move into hired lodgings; uncomfortable, inconveniently situated, and horribly expensive. Take Toad. I say nothing against Toad Hall; quite the best house in these parts, AS a house. But supposing a fire breaks out—where's Toad? Supposing tiles are blown off, or walls sink or crack, or windows get broken—where's Toad? Supposing the rooms are draughty—I HATE a draught myself—where's Toad? No, up and out of doors is good enough to roam about and get one's living in; but underground to come back to at last—that's my idea of HOME.'

The Mole assented heartily; and the Badger in consequence got very friendly with him. 'When lunch is over,' he said, 'I'll take you all round this little place of mine. I can see you'll appreciate it. You understand what domestic architecture ought to be, you do.'

After luncheon, accordingly, when the other two had settled themselves into the chimney-corner and had started a heated argument on the subject of EELS, the Badger lighted a lantern and bade the Mole follow him. Crossing the hall, they passed down one of the principal tunnels, and the wavering light of the lantern gave glimpses on either side of rooms both large and small, some mere cupboards, others nearly as broad and imposing as Toad's dining-hall. A narrow passage at right angles led them into another corridor, and here the same thing was repeated. The Mole was staggered at the size, the extent, the ramifications of it all; at the length of the dim passages, the solid vaultings of the crammed store-chambers, the masonry everywhere, the pillars, the arches, the pavements. 'How on earth, Badger,' he said at last, 'did you ever find time and strength to do all this? It's astonishing!'

'It WOULD be astonishing indeed,' said the Badger simply, 'if I HAD done it. But as a matter of fact I did none of it—only cleaned out the passages and chambers, as far as I had need of them. There's lots more of it, all round about. I see you don't understand, and I must explain it to you. Well, very long ago, on the spot where the Wild Wood waves now, before ever it had planted itself and grown up to what it now is, there was a city—a city of people, you know. Here, where we are standing, they lived, and walked, and talked, and slept, and carried on their business. Here they stabled their horses and feasted, from here they rode out to fight or drove out to trade. They were a powerful people, and rich, and great builders. They built to last, for they thought their city would last for ever.'

'But what has become of them all?' asked the Mole.

'Who can tell?' said the Badger. 'People come—they stay for a while, they flourish, they build—and they go. It is their way. But we remain. There were badgers here, I've been told, long before that same city ever came to be. And now there are badgers here again. We are an enduring lot, and we may move out for a time, but we wait, and are patient, and back we come. And so it will ever be.'

'Well, and when they went at last, those people?' said the Mole.

'When they went,' continued the Badger, 'the strong winds and persistent rains took the matter in hand, patiently, ceaselessly, year after year. Perhaps we badgers too, in our small way, helped a little—who knows? It was all down, down, down, gradually—ruin and levelling and disappearance. Then it was all up, up, up, gradually, as seeds grew to saplings, and saplings to forest trees, and bramble and fern came creeping in to help. Leaf-mould rose and obliterated, streams in their winter freshets brought sand and soil to clog and to cover, and in course of time our home was ready for us again, and we moved in. Up above us, on the surface, the same thing happened. Animals arrived, liked the look of the place, took up their quarters, settled down, spread, and flourished. They didn't bother themselves about the past—they never do; they're too busy. The place was a bit humpy and hillocky, naturally, and full of holes; but that was rather an advantage. And they don't bother about the future, either—the future when perhaps the people will move in again—for a time—as may very well be. The Wild Wood is pretty well populated by now; with all the usual lot, good, bad, and indifferent—I name no names. It takes all sorts to make a world. But I fancy you know something about them yourself by this time.'

'I do indeed,' said the Mole, with a slight shiver.

'Well, well,' said the Badger, patting him on the shoulder, 'it was your first experience of them, you see. They're not so bad really; and we must all live and let live. But I'll pass the word around to-morrow, and I think you'll have no further trouble. Any friend of MINE walks where he likes in this country, or I'll know the reason why!'

When they got back to the kitchen again, they found the Rat walking up and down, very restless. The underground atmosphere was oppressing him and getting on his nerves, and he seemed really to be afraid that the river would run away if he wasn't there to look after it. So he had his overcoat on, and his pistols thrust into his belt again. 'Come along, Mole,' he said anxiously, as soon as he caught sight of them. 'We must get off while it's daylight. Don't want to spend another night in the Wild Wood again.'

'It'll be all right, my fine fellow,' said the Otter. 'I'm coming along with you, and I know every path blindfold; and if there's a head that needs to be punched, you can confidently rely upon me to punch it.'

'You really needn't fret, Ratty,' added the Badger placidly. 'My passages run further than you think, and I've bolt-holes to the edge of the wood in several directions, though I don't care for everybody to know about them. When you really have to go, you shall leave by one of my short cuts. Meantime, make yourself easy, and sit down again.'

The Rat was nevertheless still anxious to be off and attend to his river, so the Badger, taking up his lantern again, led the way along a damp and airless tunnel that wound and dipped, part vaulted, part hewn through solid rock, for a weary distance that seemed to be miles. At last daylight began to show itself confusedly through tangled growth overhanging the mouth of the passage; and the Badger, bidding them a hasty good-bye, pushed them hurriedly through the opening, made everything look as natural as possible again, with creepers, brushwood, and dead leaves, and retreated.

They found themselves standing on the very edge of the Wild Wood. Rocks and brambles and tree-roots behind them, confusedly heaped and tangled; in front, a great space of quiet fields, hemmed by lines of hedges black on the snow, and, far ahead, a glint of the familiar old river, while the wintry sun hung red and low on the horizon. The Otter, as knowing all the paths, took charge of the party, and they trailed out on a bee-line for a distant stile. Pausing there a moment and looking back, they saw the whole mass of the Wild Wood, dense, menacing, compact, grimly set in vast white surroundings; simultaneously they turned and made swiftly for home, for firelight and the familiar things it played on, for the voice, sounding cheerily outside their window, of the river that they knew and trusted in all its moods, that never made them afraid with any amazement.

As he hurried along, eagerly anticipating the moment when he would be at home again among the things he knew and liked, the Mole saw clearly that he was an animal of tilled field and hedge-row, linked to the ploughed furrow, the frequented pasture, the lane of evening lingerings, the cultivated garden-plot. For others the asperities, the stubborn endurance, or the clash of actual conflict, that went with Nature in the rough; he must be wise, must keep to the pleasant places in which his lines were laid and which held adventure enough, in their way, to last for a lifetime.

The Pied Piper of Hamelin

ROBERT BROWNING

I

Hamelin Town's in Brunswick,
By famous Hanover city;
The river Weser, deep and wide,
Washes its wall on the southern side;
A pleasanter spot you never spied;
But, when begins my ditty,
Almost five hundred years ago,
To see the townsfolk suffer so
From vermin, was a pity.

II

Rats!
They fought the dogs and killed the cats,
And bit the babies in the cradles,
And ate the cheeses out of the vats.
And licked the soup from the cook's own ladles,
Split open the kegs of salted sprats,
Made nests inside men's Sunday hats,
And even spoiled the women's chats,
By drowning their speaking
With shrieking and squeaking

In fifty different sharps and flats.

III

At last the people in a body
To the Town Hall came flocking:
'Tis clear,' cried they, 'our Mayor's a noddy;
And as for our Corporation—shocking
To think we buy gowns lined with ermine
For dolts that can't or won't determine
What's best to rid us of our vermin!
You hope, because you're old and obese,
To find in the furry civic robe ease?
Rouse up, sirs! Give your brains a racking
To find the remedy we're lacking,
Or, sure as fate, we'll send you packing!'
At this the Mayor and Corporation
Quaked with a mighty consternation.

IV

An hour they sate in council,
At length the Mayor broke silence:
'For a guilder I'd my ermine gown sell;
I wish I were a mile hence!
It's easy to bid one rack one's brain—
I'm sure my poor head aches again,
I've scratched it so, and all in vain
Oh for a trap, a trap, a trap!'
Just as he said this, what should hap
At the chamber door but a gentle tap?
'Bless us,' cried the Mayor, 'what's that?'
(With the Corporation as he sat,

Looking little though wondrous fat;
Nor brighter was his eye, nor moister
Than a too-long-opened oyster,
Save when at noon his paunch grew mutinous
For a plate of turtle green and glutinous)
'Only a scraping of shoes on the mat?
Anything like the sound of a rat
Makes my heart go pit-a-pat!'

V

'Come in!'—the Mayor cried, looking bigger:
And in did come the strangest figure!
His queer long coat from heel to head
Was half of yellow and half of red,
And he himself was tall and thin,
With sharp blue eyes, each like a pin,
And light loose hair, yet swarthy skin
No tuft on cheek nor beard on chin,
But lips where smile went out and in;
There was no guessing his kith and kin:
And nobody could enough admire
The tall man and his quaint attire.
Quoth one: 'It's as my great-grandsire,
Starting up at the Trump of Doom's tone,
Had walked this way from his painted tombstone!'

VI

He advanced to the council-table:
And, 'Please your honours,' said he, 'I'm able,
By means of a secret charm, to draw
All creatures living beneath the sun,

That creep or swim or fly or run,
After me so as you never saw!
And I chiefly use my charm
On creatures that do people harm,
The mole and toad and newt and viper;
And people call me the Pied Piper.'
(And here they noticed round his neck
A scarf of red and yellow stripe,
To match with his coat of the self-same cheque;
And at the scarf's end hung a pipe;
And his fingers they noticed were ever straying
As if impatient to be playing
Upon his pipe, as low it dangled
Over his vesture so old-fangled.)
'Yet,' said he, 'poor Piper as I am,
In Tartary I freed the Cham,
Last June, from his huge swarms of gnats,
I eased in Asia the Nizam
Of a monstrous brood of vampyre-bats:
And as for what your brain bewilders,
If I can rid your town of rats
Will you give me a thousand guilders?'
'One? fifty thousand!'—was the exclamation
Of the astonished Mayor and Corporation.

VII

Into the street the Piper stept,
Smiling first a little smile,
As if he knew what magic slept
In his quiet pipe the while;

Then, like a musical adept,
To blow the pipe his lips he wrinkled,
And green and blue his sharp eyes twinkled,
Like a candle-flame where salt is sprinkled;
And ere three shrill notes the pipe uttered,
You heard as if an army muttered;
And the muttering grew to a grumbling;
And the grumbling grew to a mighty rumbling;
And out of the houses the rats came tumbling.
Great rats, small rats, lean rats, brawny rats,
Brown rats, black rats, grey rats, tawny rats,
Grave old plodders, gay young friskers,
Fathers, mothers, uncles, cousins,
Cocking tails and pricking whiskers,
Families by tens and dozens,
Brothers, sisters, husbands, wives—
Followed the Piper for their lives.
From street to street he piped advancing,
And step for step they followed dancing,
Until they came to the river Weser
Wherein all plunged and perished!
Save one who, stout as Julius Caesar,
Swam across and lived to carry
(As he, the manuscript he cherished)
To Rat-land home his commentary:
Which was, 'At the first shrill notes of the pipe,
I heard a sound as of scraping tripe,
And putting apples, wondrous ripe,
Into a cider-press's gripe:
And a moving away of pickle-tub-boards,
And a leaving ajar of conserve-cupboards,

And a drawing the corks of train-oil-flasks,
And a breaking the hoops of butter-casks:
And it seemed as if a voice
(Sweeter far than by harp or by psaltery
Is breathed) called out, 'Oh rats, rejoice!
The world is grown to one vast drysaltery!
So munch on, crunch on, take your nuncheon,
Breakfast, supper, dinner, luncheon!'
And just as a bulky sugar-puncheon,
All ready staved, like a great sun shone
Glorious scarce an inch before me,
Just as methought it said, 'Come, bore me!'
I found the Weser rolling o'er me.'

VIII

You should have heard the Hamelin people
Ringing the bells till they rocked the steeple
'Go,' cried the Mayor, 'and get long poles,
Poke out the nests and block up the holes!
Consult with carpenters and builders,
And leave in our town not even a trace
Of the rats!'—when suddenly up the face
Of the Piper perked in the market-place,
With a, 'First, if you please, my thousand guilders!'

IX

A thousand guilders! The Mayor looked blue;
So did the Corporation too.
For council dinners made rare havoc
With Claret, Moselle, Vin-de-Grave, Hock;
And half the money would replenish

Their cellar's biggest butt with Rhenish.
To pay this sum to a wandering fellow
With a gipsy coat of red and yellow!
'Beside,' quoth the Mayor with a knowing wink,
'Our business was done at the river's brink;
We saw with our eyes the vermin sink,
And what's dead can't come to life, I think.
So, friend, we're not the folks to shrink
From the duty of giving you something to drink,
And a matter of money to put in your poke;
But as for the guilders, what we spoke
Of them, as you very well know, was in joke.
Beside, our losses have made us thrifty.
A thousand guilders! Come, take fifty!'

X

The Piper's face fell, and he cried,
'No trifling! I can't wait, beside!
I've promised to visit by dinner-time
Bagdad, and accept the prime
Of the Head-Cook's pottage, all he's rich in,
For having left, in the Caliph's kitchen,
Of a nest of scorpions no survivor:
With him I proved no bargain-driver,
With you, don't think I'll bate a stiver!
And folks who put me in a passion
May find me pipe after another fashion.'

XI

'How?' cried the Mayor, 'd' ye think I brook
Being worse treated than a Cook?

Insulted by a lazy ribald
With idle pipe and vesture piebald?
You threaten us, fellow? Do your worst,
Blow your pipe there till you burst!'

XII

Once more he stept into the street,
And to his lips again
Laid his long pipe of smooth straight cane;
And ere he blew three notes
(such sweet
Soft notes as yet musician's cunning
Never gave the enraptured air)
There was a rustling,
that seemed like a bustling
Of merry crowds justling at pitching and hustling,
Small feet were pattering, wooden shoes clattering,
Little hands clapping and little tongues chattering,
And, like fowls in a farm-yard when barley is scattering,
Out came the children running.
All the little boys and girls,
With rosy cheeks and flaxen curls,
And sparkling eyes and teeth like pearls.
Tripping
And skipping,
Ran merrily after
The wonderful music with shouting and laughter.

XIII

The Mayor was dumb, and the Council stood
As if they were changed into blocks of wood,

Unable to move a step, or cry
To the children merrily skipping by.
Could only follow with the eye
That joyous crowd at the Piper's back.
But how the Mayor was on the rack,
And the wretched Council's bosoms beat,
As the Piper turned from the High Street
To where the Weser rolled its waters
Right in the way of their sons and daughters!
However he turned from South to West,
And to Koppelberg Hill his steps addressed,
And after him the children pressed;
Great was the joy in every breast.
'He never can cross that mighty top!
He's forced to let the piping drop,
And we shall see our children stop!'
When, lo, as they reached the mountain-side,
A wondrous portal opened wide,
As if a cavern was suddenly hollowed;
And the Piper advanced and the children followed,
And when all were in to the very last,
The door in the mountain side shut fast.
Did I say, all? No; One was lame,
And could not dance the whole of the way;
And in after years, if you would blame
His sadness, he was used to say,—
'It's dull in our town since my playmates left!
I can't forget that I'm bereft
Of all the pleasant sights they see,
Which the Piper also promised me.
For he led us, he said, to a joyous land,

Joining the town and just at hand,
Where waters gushed and fruit-trees grew,
And flowers put forth a fairer hue,
And everything was strange and new;
The sparrows were brighter than peacocks here,
And their dogs outran our fallow deer,
And honey-bees had lost their stings,
And horses were born with eagles' wings;
And just as I became assured
My lame foot would be speedily cured,
The music stopped and I stood still,
And found myself outside the hill,
Left alone against my will,
To go now limping as before,
And never hear of that country more!'

XIV

Alas, alas for Hamelin!
There came into many a burgher's pate
A text which says that Heaven's gate
Opes to the rich at as easy rate
As the needle's eye takes a camel in!
The Mayor sent East, West, North, and South,
To offer the Piper, by word of mouth,
Wherever it was men's lot to find him,
Silver and gold to his heart's content,
If he'd only return the way he went,
And bring the children behind him.
But when they saw 'twas a lost endeavour,
And Piper and dancers were gone for ever,
They made a decree that lawyers never

Should think their records dated duly
If, after the day of the month and year,
These words did not as well appear,
'And so long after what happened here
On the Twenty-second of July,
Thirteen hundred and seventy-six:'
And the better in memory to fix
The place of the children's last retreat,
They called it, the Pied Piper's Street—
Where any one playing on pipe or tabor,
Was sure for the future to lose his labour.
Nor suffered they hostelry or tavern
To shock with mirth a street so solemn;
But opposite the place of the cavern
They wrote the story on a column,
And on the great church-window painted
The same, to make the world acquainted
How their children were stolen away,
And there it stands to this very day.
And I must not omit to say
That in Transylvania there's a tribe
Of alien people that ascribe
The outlandish ways and dress
On which their neighbours lay such stress,
To their fathers and mothers having risen
Out of some subterraneous prison
Into which they were trepanned
Long time ago in a mighty band
Out of Hamelin town in Brunswick land,
But how or why, they don't understand.

XV

So, Willy, let me and you be wipers
Of scores out with all men—especially pipers!
And, whether they pipe us free from rats or from mice,
If we've promised them aught, let us keep our promise!

A School Story

M.R. JAMES

Two men in a smoking-room were talking of their private-school days. 'At *our* school,' said A., 'we had a ghost's footmark on the staircase. What was it like? Oh, very unconvincing. Just the shape of a shoe, with a square toe, if I remember right. The staircase was a stone one. I never heard any story about the thing. That seems odd, when you come to think of it. Why didn't somebody invent one, I wonder?'

'You never can tell with little boys. They have a mythology of their own. There's a subject for you, by the way—'The Folklore of Private Schools.'

'Yes; the crop is rather scanty, though. I imagine, if you were to investigate the cycle of ghost stories, for instance, which the boys at private schools tell each other, they would all turn out to be highly-compressed versions of stories out of books.'

'Nowadays the *Strand* and *Pearson's*, and so on, would be extensively drawn upon.'

'No doubt: they weren't born or thought of in *my* time. Let's see. I wonder if I can remember the staple ones that I was told. First, there was the house with a room in which a series of people insisted on passing a night; and each of them in the morning was found kneeling in a corner, and had just time to say, "I've seen it," and died.'

'Wasn't that the house in Berkeley Square?'

'I dare say it was. Then there was the man who heard a noise in the passage at night, opened his door, and saw someone crawling towards him on all fours with his eye hanging out on his cheek. There was besides, let me think—Yes! the room where a man was found dead in bed with a horseshoe mark on his forehead, and the floor under the bed was covered with marks of horseshoes also; I don't know why. Also there was the lady who, on locking her bedroom door in a strange house, heard a thin voice among the bed-curtains say, "Now we're shut in for the night." None of those had any explanation or sequel. I wonder if they go on still, those stories.'

'Oh, likely enough—with additions from the magazines, as I said. You never heard, did you, of a real ghost at a private school? I thought not; nobody has that ever I came across.'

'From the way in which you said that, I gather that *you* have.'

'I really don't know; but this is what was in my mind. It happened at my private school thirty odd years ago, and I haven't any explanation of it.

'The school I mean was near London. It was established in a large and fairly old house—a great white building with very fine grounds about it; there were large cedars in the garden, as there are in so many of the older gardens in the Thames valley, and ancient elms in the three or four fields which we used for our games. I think probably it was quite an attractive place, but boys seldom allow that their schools possess any tolerable features.

'I came to the school in a September, soon after the year 1870; and among the boys who arrived on the same day was one whom I took to: a Highland boy, whom I will call McLeod. I needn't spend time in describing him: the main thing is that

I got to know him very well. He was not an exceptional boy in any way—not particularly good at books or games—but he suited me.

'The school was a large one: there must have been from 120 to 130 boys there as a rule, and so a considerable staff of masters was required, and there were rather frequent changes among them.

'One term—perhaps it was my third or fourth—a new master made his appearance. His name was Sampson. He was a tallish, stoutish, pale, black-bearded man. I think we liked him: he had travelled a good deal, and had stories which amused us on our school walks, so that there was some competition among us to get within earshot of him. I remember too—dear me, I have hardly thought of it since then!—that he had a charm on his watch-chain that attracted my attention one day, and he let me examine it. It was, I now suppose, a gold Byzantine coin; there was an effigy of some absurd emperor on one side; the other side had been worn practically smooth, and he had had cut on it—rather barbarously—his own initials, G.W.S., and a date, 24 July 1865. Yes, I can see it now: he told me he had picked it up in Constantinople: it was about the size of a florin, perhaps rather smaller.

'Well, the first odd thing that happened was this. Sampson was doing Latin grammar with us. One of his favourite methods—perhaps it is rather a good one—was to make us construct sentences out of our own heads to illustrate the rules he was trying to make us learn. Of course that is a thing which gives a silly boy a chance of being impertinent: there are lots of school stories in which that happens—or anyhow there might be. But Sampson was too good a disciplinarian for us to think of trying that on with him. Now, on this occasion he was telling us how to express *remembering* in Latin: and he ordered us each to make a sentence bringing in the verb *memini*, "I remember." Well, most of us made up some ordinary sentence such as "I remember my father," or "He remembers his book," or something equally uninteresting: and I dare say a good many put down *memino librum meum*, and so forth: but the boy I mentioned—McLeod—was evidently thinking of something more elaborate than that. The rest of us wanted to have our sentences passed, and get on to something else, so some kicked him under the desk, and I, who was next to him, poked him and whispered to him to look sharp. But he didn't seem to attend. I looked at his paper and saw he had put down nothing at all. So I jogged him again harder than before and upbraided him sharply for keeping us all waiting. That did have some effect. He started and seemed to wake up, and then very quickly he scribbled about a couple of lines on his paper, and showed it up with the rest. As it was the last, or nearly the last, to come in, and as Sampson had a good deal to say to the boys who had written *meminiscimus patri meo* and the rest of it, it turned out that the clock struck twelve before he had got to McLeod, and McLeod had to wait afterwards to have his sentence corrected. There was nothing much going on outside when I got out, so I waited for him to come. He came very slowly when he did arrive, and I guessed there had been some sort of trouble. "Well," I said, "what did you get?" "Oh, I don't know," said McLeod, "nothing much: but I think Sampson's rather sick with me." "Why, did you show him up some rot?" "No fear," he said. "It was all right as far as I could see: it was like this: *Memento*—that's right enough for remember, and it takes a genitive,—*memento putei inter quatuor taxos.*" "What silly rot!" I said. "What made you shove that down? What does it mean?"

"That's the funny part," said McLeod. "I'm not quite sure what it does mean. All I know is, it just came into my head and I corked it down. I know what I *think* it means, because just before I wrote it down I had a sort of picture of it in my head: I believe it means 'Remember the well among the four'—what are those dark sort of trees that have red berries on them?" "Mountain ashes, I s'pose you mean." "I never heard of them," said McLeod; "no, *I'll* tell you—yews." "Well, and what did Sampson say?" "Why, he was jolly odd about it. When he read it he got up and went to the mantelpiece and stopped quite a long time without saying anything, with his back to me. And then he said, without turning round, and rather quiet, 'What do you suppose that means?' I told him what I thought; only I couldn't remember the name of the silly tree: and then he wanted to know why I put it down, and I had to say something or other. And after that he left off talking about it, and asked me how long I'd been here, and where my people lived, and things like that: and then I came away: but he wasn't looking a bit well."

'I don't remember any more that was said by either of us about this. Next day McLeod took to his bed with a chill or something of the kind, and it was a week or more before he was in school again. And as much as a month went by without anything happening that was noticeable. Whether or not Mr Sampson was really startled, as McLeod had thought, he didn't show it. I am pretty sure, of course, now, that there was something very curious in his past history, but I'm not going to pretend that we boys were sharp enough to guess any such thing.

'There was one other incident of the same kind as the last which I told you. Several times since that day we had had to make up examples in school to illustrate different rules, but there had never been any row except when we did them wrong. At last there came a day when we were going through those dismal things which people call conditional sentences, and we were told to make a conditional sentence, expressing a future consequence. We did it, right or wrong, and showed up our bits of paper, and Sampson began looking through them. All at once he got up, made some odd sort of noise in his throat, and rushed out by a door that was just by his desk. We sat there for a minute or two, and then—I suppose it was incorrect—but we went up, I and one or two others, to look at the papers on his desk. Of course I thought someone must have put down some nonsense or other, and Sampson had gone off to report him. All the same, I noticed that he hadn't taken any of the papers with him when he ran out. Well, the top paper on the desk was written in red ink—which no one used—and it wasn't in anyone's hand who was in the class. They all looked at it—McLeod and all—and took their dying oaths that it wasn't theirs. Then I thought of counting the bits of paper. And of this I made quite certain: that there were seventeen bits of paper on the desk, and sixteen boys in the form. Well, I bagged the extra paper, and kept it, and I believe I have it now. And now you will want to know what was written on it. It was simple enough, and harmless enough, I should have said.

'"*Si tu non veneris ad me, ego veniam ad te*," which means, I suppose, "If you don't come to me, I'll come to you."

'Could you show me the paper?' interrupted the listener.

'Yes, I could: but there's another odd thing about it. That same afternoon I took it out of my locker—I know for certain it was the same bit, for I made a finger-mark on it—and no single trace of writing of any kind was there on it. I kept it, as I said, and since that time I have tried various experiments to see whether sympathetic ink had been used, but absolutely without result.

'So much for that. After about half an hour Sampson looked in again: said he had felt very unwell, and told us we might go. He came rather gingerly to his desk, and gave just one look at the uppermost paper: and I suppose he thought he must have been dreaming: anyhow, he asked no questions.

'That day was a half-holiday, and next day Sampson was in school again, much as usual. That night the third and last incident in my story happened.

'We—McLeod and I—slept in a dormitory at right angles to the main building. Sampson slept in the main building on the first floor. There was a very bright full moon. At an hour which I can't tell exactly, but some time between one and two, I was woken up by somebody shaking me. It was McLeod; and a nice state of mind he seemed to be in. "Come," he said,—"come! there's a burglar getting in through Sampson's window." As soon as I could speak, I said, "Well, why not call out and wake everybody up?" "No, no," he said, "I'm not sure who it is: don't make a row: come and look." Naturally I came and looked, and naturally there was no one there. I was cross enough, and should have called McLeod plenty of names: only—I couldn't tell why—it seemed to me that there *was* something wrong—something that made me very glad I wasn't alone to face it. We were still at the window looking out, and as soon as I could, I asked him what he had heard or seen. "I didn't *hear* anything at all," he said, "but about five minutes before I woke you, I found myself looking out of this window here, and there was a man sitting or kneeling on Sampson's window-sill, and looking in, and I thought he was beckoning." "What sort of man?" McLeod wriggled. "I don't know," he said, "but I can tell you one thing—he was beastly thin: and he looked as if he was wet all over: and," he said, looking round and whispering as if he hardly liked to hear himself, "I'm not at all sure that he was alive."

'We went on talking in whispers some time longer, and eventually crept back to bed. No one else in the room woke or stirred the whole time. I believe we did sleep a bit afterwards, but we were very cheap next day.

'And next day Mr Sampson was gone: not to be found: and I believe no trace of him has ever come to light since. In thinking it over, one of the oddest things about it all has seemed to me to be the fact that neither McLeod nor I ever mentioned what we had seen to any third person whatever. Of course no questions were asked on the subject, and if they had been, I am inclined to believe that we could not have made any answer: we seemed unable to speak about it.

'That is my story,' said the narrator. 'The only approach to a ghost story connected with a school that I know, but still, I think, an approach to such a thing.'

The sequel to this may perhaps be reckoned highly conventional; but a sequel there is, and so it must be produced. There had been more than one listener to the story, and, in the latter part of that same year, or of the next, one such listener was staying at a country house in Ireland.

One evening his host was turning over a drawer full of odds and ends in the smoking-room. Suddenly he put his hand upon a little box. 'Now,' he said, 'you know about old things; tell me what that is.' My friend opened the little box, and found in it a thin gold chain with an object attached to it. He glanced at the object and then took off his spectacles to examine it more narrowly. 'What's the history of this?' he asked. 'Odd enough,' was the answer. 'You know the yew thicket in the shrubbery: well, a year or two back we were cleaning out the old well that used to be in the clearing here, and what do you suppose we found?'

'Is it possible that you found a body?' said the visitor, with an odd feeling of nervousness.

'We did that: but what's more, in every sense of the word, we found two.'

'Good Heavens! Two? Was there anything to show how they got there? Was this thing found with them?'

'It was. Amongst the rags of the clothes that were on one of the bodies. A bad business, whatever the story of it may have been. One body had the arms tight round the other. They must have been there thirty years or more—long enough before we came to this place. You may judge we filled the well up fast enough. Do you make anything of what's cut on that gold coin you have there?'

'I think I can,' said my friend, holding it to the light (but he read it without much difficulty); 'it seems to be G.W.S., 24 July 1865.'

Jeeves Exerts the Old Cerebellum

P.G. WODEHOUSE

'Morning, Jeeves,' I said.

'Good morning, sir,' said Jeeves. He put the good old cup of tea softly on the table by my bed, and I took a refreshing sip. Just right, as usual. Not too hot, not too sweet, not too weak, not too strong, not too much milk, and not a drop spilled in the saucer. A most amazing cove, Jeeves. So dashed competent in every respect. I've said it before, and I'll say it again. I mean to say, take just one small instance. Every other valet I've ever had used to barge into my room in the morning while I was still asleep, causing much misery: but Jeeves seems to know when I'm awake by a sort of telepathy. He always floats in with the cup exactly two minutes after I come to life. Makes a deuce of a lot of difference to a fellow's day.

'How's the weather, Jeeves?'

'Exceptionally clement, sir.'

'Anything in the papers?'

'Some slight friction threatening in the Balkans, sir. Otherwise, nothing.'

'I say, Jeeves, a man I met at the club last night told me to put my shirt on Privateer for the two o'clock race this afternoon. How about it?'

'I should not advocate it, sir. The stable is not sanguine.'

That was enough for me. Jeeves knows. How, I couldn't say, but he knows. There was a time when I would laugh lightly, and go ahead, and lose my little all against his advice, but not now.

'Talking of shirts,' I said, 'have those mauve ones I ordered arrived yet?'

'Yes, sir. I sent them back.'

'Sent them back?'

'Yes, sir. They would not have become you.'

Well, I must say I'd thought fairly highly of those shirtings, but I bowed to superior knowledge. Weak? I don't know. Most fellows, no doubt, are all for having their valets confine their activities to creasing trousers and what not without trying to run the home; but it's different with Jeeves. Right from the first day he came to me, I have looked on him as a sort of guide, philosopher, and friend.

'Mr Little rang up on the telephone a few moments ago, sir. I informed him that you were not yet awake.'

'Did he leave a message?'

'No, sir. He mentioned that he had a matter of importance to discuss with you, but confided no details.'

'Oh, well, I expect I shall be seeing him at the club.'

'No doubt, sir.'

I wasn't what you might call in a fever of impatience. Bingo Little is a chap I was at school with, and we see a lot of each other still. He's the nephew of old Mortimer Little, who retired from business recently with a goodish pile. (You've probably heard of Little's Liniment—It Limbers Up the Legs.) Bingo biffs about London on a pretty comfortable allowance given him by his uncle, and leads on the whole a fairly unclouded life. It wasn't likely that anything which he described as a matter of importance would turn out to be really so frightfully important.

I took it that he had discovered some new brand of cigarette which he wanted me to try, or something like that, and didn't spoil my breakfast by worrying.

After breakfast I lit a cigarette and went to the open window to inspect the day. It certainly was one of the best and brightest.

'Jeeves,' I said.

'Sir?' said Jeeves. He had been clearing away the breakfast things, but at the sound of the young master's voice cheesed it courteously.

'You were absolutely right about the weather. It is a juicy morning.'

'Decidedly, sir.'

'Spring and all that.'

'Yes, sir.'

'In the spring, Jeeves, a livelier iris gleams upon the burnished dove.'

'So I have been informed, sir.'

'Right ho! Then bring me my whangee, my yellowest shoes, and the old green Homburg. I'm going into the Park to do pastoral dances.'

I don't know if you know that sort of feeling you get on these days round about the end of April and the beginning of May, when the sky's a light blue, with cotton-wool clouds, and there's a bit of a breeze blowing from the west? Kind of uplifted feeling. Romantic, if you know what I mean. I'm not much of a ladies' man, but on this particular morning it seemed to me that what I really wanted was some charming girl to buzz up and ask me to save her from assassins or something. So that it was a bit of an anti-climax when I merely ran into young Bingo Little, looking perfectly foul in a crimson satin tie decorated with horseshoes.

'Hallo, Bertie,' said Bingo.

'My God, man!' I gargled. 'The cravat! The gent's neckwear! Why? For what reason?'

'Oh, the tie?' He blushed. 'I—er—I was given it.'

He seemed embarrassed, so I dropped the subject. We toddled along a bit, and sat down on a couple of chairs by the Serpentine.

'Jeeves tells me you want to talk to me about something,' I said.

'Eh?' said Bingo, with a start. 'Oh yes, yes. Yes.'

I waited for him to unleash the topic of the day, but he didn't seem to want to get going. Conversation languished. He stared straight ahead of him in a glassy sort of manner.

'I say, Bertie,' he said, after a pause of about an hour and a quarter.

'Hallo!'

'Do you like the name Mabel?'

'No.'

'No?'

'No.'

'You don't think there's a kind of music in the word, like the wind rustling gently through the tree-tops?'

'No.'

He seemed disappointed for a moment; then cheered up.

'Of course, you wouldn't. You always were a fat-headed worm without any soul, weren't you?'

'Just as you say. Who is she? Tell me all.'

For I realized now that poor old Bingo was going through it once again. Ever since I have known him—and we were at school together—he has been perpetually falling in love with someone, generally in the spring, which seems to act on him like magic. At school he had the finest collection of actresses' photographs of anyone of his time; and at Oxford his romantic nature was a byword.

'You'd better come along and meet her at lunch,' he said, looking at his watch.

'A ripe suggestion,' I said. 'Where are you meeting her? At the Ritz?'

'Near the Ritz.'

He was geographically accurate. About fifty yards east of the Ritz there is one of those blighted tea-and-bun shops you see dotted about all over London, and into this, if you'll believe me, young Bingo dived like a homing rabbit; and before I had time to say a word we were wedged in at a table, on the brink of a silent pool of coffee left there by an early luncher.

I'm bound to say I couldn't quite follow the development of the scenario. Bingo, while not absolutely rolling in the stuff, has always had a fair amount of the ready. Apart from what he got from his uncle, I knew that he had finished up the jumping season well on the right side of the ledger. Why, then, was he lunching the girl at this Godforsaken eatery? It couldn't be because he was hard up.

Just then the waitress arrived. Rather a pretty girl.

'Aren't we going to wait——?' I started to say to Bingo, thinking it somewhat thick that, in addition to asking a girl to lunch with him in a place like this, he should fling himself on the foodstuffs before she turned up, when I caught sight of his face, and stopped.

The man was goggling. His entire map was suffused with a rich blush. He looked like the Soul's Awakening done in pink.

'Hallo, Mabel!' he said, with a sort of gulp.

'Hallo!' said the girl.

'Mabel,' said Bingo, 'this is Bertie Wooster, a pal of mine.'

'Pleased to meet you,' she said. 'Nice morning.'

'Fine,' I said.

'You see I'm wearing the tie,' said Bingo.

'It suits you beautiful,' said the girl.

Personally, if anyone had told me that a tie like that suited me, I should have risen and struck them on the mazzard, regardless of their age and sex; but poor old Bingo simply got all flustered with gratification, and smirked in the most gruesome manner.

'Well, what's it going to be to-day?' asked the girl, introducing the business touch into the conversation.

Bingo studied the menu devoutly.

'I'll have a cup of cocoa, cold veal and ham pie, slice of fruit cake, and a macaroon. Same for you, Bertie?'

I gazed at the man, revolted. That he could have been a pal of mine all these years and think me capable of insulting the old tum with this sort of stuff cut me to the quick.

'Or how about a bit of hot steak-pudding, with a sparkling limado to wash it down?' said Bingo.

You know, the way love can change a fellow is really frightful to contemplate. This chappie before me, who spoke in that absolutely careless way of macaroons and limado, was the man I had seen in happier days telling the head-waiter at Claridge's exactly how he wanted the *chef* to prepare the *sole frite au gourmet aux champignons*, and saying he would jolly well sling it back if it wasn't just right. Ghastly! Ghastly!

A roll and butter and a small coffee seemed the only things on the list that hadn't been specially prepared by the nastier-minded members of the Borgia family for people they had a particular grudge against, so I chose them, and Mabel hopped it.

'Well?' said Bingo rapturously.

I took it that he wanted my opinion of the female poisoner who had just left us.

'Very nice,' I said.

He seemed dissatisfied.

'You don't think she's the most wonderful girl you ever saw?' he said wistfully.

'Oh, absolutely!' I said, to appease the blighter. 'Where did you meet her?'

'At a subscription dance at Camberwell.'

'What on earth were you doing at a subscription dance at Camberwell?'

'Your man Jeeves asked me if I would buy a couple of tickets. It was in aid of some charity or other.'

'Jeeves? I didn't know he went in for that sort of thing.'

'Well, I suppose he has to relax a bit every now and then. Anyway, he was there, swinging a dashed efficient shoe. I hadn't meant to go at first, but I turned up for a lark. Oh, Bertie, think what I might have missed!'

'What might you have missed?' I asked, the old lemon being slightly clouded.

'Mabel, you chump. If I hadn't gone I shouldn't have met Mabel.'

'Oh, ah!'

At this point Bingo fell into a species of trance, and only came out of it to wrap himself round the pie and macaroon.

'Bertie,' he said, 'I want your advice.'

'Carry on.'

'At least, not your advice, because that wouldn't be much good to anybody. I mean, you're a pretty consummate old ass, aren't you? Not that I want to hurt your feelings, of course.'

'No, no, I see that.'

'What I wish you would do is to put the whole thing to that fellow Jeeves of yours, and see what he suggests. You've often told me that he has helped other pals of yours out of messes. From what you tell me, he's by way of being the brains of the family.'

'He's never let me down yet.'

'Then put my case to him.'

'What case?'

'My problem.'

'What problem?'

'Why, you poor fish, my uncle, of course. What do you think my uncle's going to say to all this? If I sprang it on him cold, he'd tie himself in knots on the hearthrug.'

'One of these emotional johnnies, eh?'

'Somehow or other his mind has got to be prepared to receive the news. But how?'

'Ah!'

'That's a lot of help, that 'ah'! You see, I'm pretty well dependent on the old boy. If he cut off my allowance, I should be very much in the soup. So you put the whole binge to Jeeves and see if he can't scare up a happy ending somehow. Tell him my future is in his hands, and that, if the wedding bells ring out, he can rely on me, even unto half my kingdom. Well, call it ten quid. Jeeves would exert himself with ten quid on the horizon, what?'

'Undoubtedly,' I said.

I wasn't in the least surprised at Bingo wanting to lug Jeeves into his private affairs like this. It was the first thing I would have thought of doing myself if I had been in any hole of any description. As I have frequently had occasion to observe, he is a bird of the ripest intellect, full of bright ideas. If anybody could fix things for poor old Bingo, he could.

I stated the case to him that night after dinner.

'Jeeves.'

'Sir?'

'Are you busy just now?'

'No, sir.'

'I mean, not doing anything in particular?'

'No, sir. It is my practice at this hour to read some improving book; but, if you desire my services, this can easily be postponed, or, indeed, abandoned altogether.'

'Well, I want your advice. It's about Mr Little.'

'Young Mr Little, sir, or the elder Mr Little, his uncle, who lives in Pounceby Gardens?'

Jeeves seemed to know everything. Most amazing thing. I'd been pally with Bingo practically all my life, and yet I didn't remember ever having heard that his uncle lived anywhere is particular.

'How did you know he lived in Pounceby Gardens?' I said.

'I am on terms of some intimacy with the elder Mr Little's cook, sir. In fact, there is an understanding.'

I'm bound to say that this gave me a bit of a start. Somehow I'd never thought of Jeeves going in for that sort of thing.

'Do you mean you're engaged?'

'It may be said to amount to that, sir.'

'Well, well!'

'She is a remarkably excellent cook, sir,' said Jeeves, as though he felt called on to give some explanation. 'What was it you wished to ask me about Mr Little?'

I sprang the details on him.

'And that's how the matter stands, Jeeves,' I said. 'I think we ought to rally round a trifle and help poor old Bingo put the thing through. Tell me about old Mr Little. What sort of a chap is he?'

'A somewhat curious character, sir. Since retiring from business he has become a great recluse, and now devotes himself almost entirely to the pleasures of the table.'

'Greedy hog, you mean?'

'I would not, perhaps, take the liberty of describing him in precisely those terms, sir. He is what is usually called a gourmet. Very particular about what he eats, and for that reason sets a high value on Miss Watson's services.'

'The cook?'

'Yes, sir.'

'Well, it looks to me as though our best plan would be to shoot young Bingo in on him after dinner one night. Melting mood, I mean to say, and all that.'

'The difficulty is, sir, that at the moment Mr Little is on a diet, owing to an attack of gout.'

'Things begin to look wobbly.'

'No, sir, I fancy that the elder Mr Little's misfortune may be turned to the younger Mr Little's advantage. I was speaking only the other day to Mr Little's valet, and he was telling me that it has become his principal duty to read to Mr Little in the evenings. If I were in your place, sir, I should send young Mr Little to read to his uncle.'

'Nephew's devotion, you mean? Old man touched by kindly action, what?'

'Partly that, sir. But I would rely more on young Mr Little's choice of literature.'

'That's no good. Jolly old Bingo has a kind face, but when it comes to literature he stops at the *Sporting Times*.'

'That difficulty may be overcome. I would be happy to select books for Mr Little to read. Perhaps I might explain my idea further?'

'I can't say I quite grasp it yet.'

'The method which I advocate is what, I believe, the advertisers call Direct Suggestion, sir, consisting as it does of driving an idea home by constant repetition. You may have had experience of the system?'

'You mean they keep on telling you that some soap or other is the best, and after a bit you come under the influence and charge round the corner and buy a cake?'

'Exactly, sir. The same method was the basis of all the most valuable propaganda during the recent war. I see no reason why it should not be adopted to bring about the desired result with regard to the subject's views on class distinctions. If young Mr Little were to read day after day to his uncle a series of narratives in which marriage with young persons of an inferior social status was held up as both feasible and admirable, I fancy it would prepare the elder Mr Little's mind for the reception of the information that his nephew wishes to marry a waitress in a tea-shop.'

'*Are* there any books of that sort nowadays? The only ones I ever see mentioned in the papers are about married couples who find life grey, and can't stick to each other at any price.'

'Yes, sir, there are a great many, neglected by the reviewers but widely read. You have never encountered 'All for Love,' by Rosie M. Banks?'

'No.'

'Nor 'A Red, Red Summer Rose,' by the same author?'

'No.'

'I have an aunt, sir, who owns an almost complete set of

Rosie M. Banks'. I could easily borrow as many volumes as young Mr Little might require. They make very light, attractive reading.'

'Well, it's worth trying.'

'I should certainly recommend the scheme, sir.'

'All right, then. Toddle round to your aunt's to-morrow and grab a couple of the fruitiest. We can but have a dash at it.'

'Precisely, sir.'

Typhoon

JOSEPH CONRAD

I

Captain MacWhirr, of the steamer Nan-Shan, had a physiognomy that, in the order of material appearances, was the exact counterpart of his mind: it presented no marked characteristics of firmness or stupidity; it had no pronounced characteristics whatever; it was simply ordinary, irresponsive and unruffled.

The only thing his aspect might have been said to suggest, at times, was bashfulness; because he would sit, in business offices ashore, sunburnt and smiling faintly, with downcast eyes. When he raised them, they were perceived to be direct in their glance and of blue colour. His hair was fair and extremely fine, clasping from temple to temple the bald dome of his skull in a clamp as of fluffy silk. The hair of his face, on the contrary, carroty and flaming, resembled a growth of copper wire clipped short to the line of the lip; while, no matter how close he shaved, fiery metallic gleams passed, when he moved his head, over the surface of his cheeks. He was rather below the medium height, a bit round-shouldered, and so sturdy of limb that his clothes always looked a shade too tight for his arms and legs. As if unable to grasp what is due to the difference of latitudes, he wore a brown bowler hat, a complete suit of a brownish hue, and clumsy black boots. These harbour togs gave to his thick figure an air of stiff and uncouth smartness. A thin silver watch chain looped his waistcoat, and he never left his ship for the shore without clutching in his powerful, hairy fist an elegant umbrella of the very best quality, but generally unrolled. Young Jukes, the chief mate, attending his commander to the gangway, would sometimes venture to say, with the greatest gentleness, 'Allow me, sir'—and possessing himself of the umbrella deferentially, would elevate the ferule, shake the folds, twirl a neat furl in a jiffy, and hand it back; going through the performance with a face of such portentous gravity, that Mr Solomon Rout, the chief engineer, smoking his morning cigar over the skylight, would turn away his head in order to hide a smile. 'Oh! aye! The blessed gamp...Thank 'ee, Jukes, thank 'ee,' would mutter Captain MacWhirr, heartily, without looking up.

Having just enough imagination to carry him through each successive day, and no more, he was tranquilly sure of himself; and from the very same cause he was not in the least conceited. It is your imaginative superior who is touchy, overbearing and difficult to please; but every ship Captain MacWhirr commanded was the floating abode of harmony and peace. It was, in truth, as impossible for him to take a flight of fancy as it would be for a watchmaker to put together a chronometer with nothing except a two-pound hammer and a whip-saw in the way of tools. Yet the uninteresting lives of men so entirely given to the actuality of the bare existence have their mysterious side. It was impossible in Captain MacWhirr's case, for instance, to understand what under heaven could have induced that perfectly satisfactory son of a petty grocer in Belfast to run away to sea. And yet he had done that very thing at the age of fifteen. It was enough, when you thought it over, to give you the idea of an immense, potent, and invisible hand thrust into the ant-heap of the earth, laying hold of shoulders, knocking heads together, and setting the unconscious faces of the multitude towards inconceivable goals and in undreamt-of directions.

His father never really forgave him for this undutiful stupidity. 'We could have got on without him,' he used to say later on, 'but there's the business. And he is an only son, too!' His mother wept very much after his disappearance. As it had never occurred to him to leave word behind, he was mourned over for dead till, after eight months, his first letter arrived from Talcahuano. It was short, and contained the statement: 'We had very fine weather on our passage out.' But evidently, in the writer's mind, the only important intelligence was to the effect that his captain had, on the very day of writing, entered him regularly on the ship's articles as Ordinary Seaman. 'Because I can do the work,' he explained. The mother again wept copiously, while the remark, 'Tom's an ass,' expressed the emotions of the father. He was a corpulent man, with a gift for sly chaffing, which to the end of his life he exercised in his intercourse with his son, a little pityingly, as if upon a half-witted person.

MacWhirr's visits to his home were necessarily rare, and in the course of years he despatched other letters to his parents, informing them of his successive promotions and of his movements upon the vast earth. In these missives could be found sentences like this: 'The heat here is very great.' Or: 'On Christmas day at 4 p.m. we fell in with some icebergs.' The old people ultimately became acquainted with a good many names of ships, and with the names of the skippers who commanded them—with the names of Scots and English shipowners—with the names of seas, oceans, straits, promontories—with outlandish names of lumber-ports, of rice-ports, of cotton-ports—with the names of islands—with the name of their son's young woman. She was called Lucy. It did not suggest itself to him to mention whether he thought the name pretty. And then they died.

The great day of MacWhirr's marriage came in due course, following shortly upon the great day when he got his first command.

All these events had taken place many years before the morning when, in the chart-room of the steamer Nan-Shan, he stood confronted by the fall of a barometer he had no reason to distrust. The fall—taking into account the excellence of the instrument, the time of the year, and the ship's position on the terrestrial globe—was of a nature ominously prophetic; but the red face of the man betrayed no sort of inward disturbance. Omens were as nothing to him, and he was unable to discover the message of a prophecy till the fulfilment had brought it home to his very door. 'That's a fall, and no mistake,' he thought. 'There must be some uncommonly dirty weather knocking about.'

The Nan-Shan was on her way from the southward to the treaty port of Fu-chau, with some cargo in her lower holds, and two hundred Chinese coolies returning to their village homes in the province of Fo-kien, after a few years of work in various tropical colonies. The morning was fine, the oily sea heaved without a sparkle, and there was a queer white misty patch in the sky like a halo of the sun. The fore-deck, packed with Chinamen, was full of sombre clothing, yellow faces, and pigtails, sprinkled over with a good many naked shoulders, for there was no wind, and the heat was close. The coolies lounged, talked, smoked, or stared over the rail; some, drawing water over the side, sluiced each other; a few slept on hatches, while several small parties of six sat on their heels surrounding iron trays with plates of rice and tiny teacups; and every single Celestial of them was carrying with him all he had in the world—a wooden chest with a ringing lock and brass on the corners, containing the savings of his labours: some clothes of ceremony, sticks of incense, a little opium maybe, bits of nameless rubbish of conventional value, and a small hoard of silver dollars, toiled for in coal lighters, won in gambling-houses or in petty trading, grubbed out of earth, sweated out in mines, on railway lines, in deadly jungle, under heavy burdens—amassed patiently, guarded with care, cherished fiercely.

A cross swell had set in from the direction of Formosa Channel about ten o'clock, without disturbing these passengers much, because the Nan-Shan, with her flat bottom, rolling chocks on bilges, and great breadth of beam, had the reputation of an exceptionally steady ship in a sea-way. Mr Jukes, in moments of expansion on shore, would proclaim loudly that the 'old girl was as good as she was pretty.' It would never have occurred to Captain MacWhirr to express his favourable opinion so loud or in terms so fanciful.

She was a good ship, undoubtedly, and not old either. She had been built in Dumbarton less than three years before, to the order of a firm of merchants in Siam—Messrs Sigg and Son. When she lay afloat, finished in every detail and ready to take up the work of her life, the builders contemplated her with pride.

'Sigg has asked us for a reliable skipper to take her out,' remarked one of the partners; and the other, after reflecting for a while, said: 'I think MacWhirr is ashore just at present.' 'Is he? Then wire him at once. He's the very man,' declared the senior, without a moment's hesitation.

Next morning MacWhirr stood before them unperturbed, having travelled from London by the midnight express after a sudden but undemonstrative parting with his wife. She was the daughter of a superior couple who had seen better days.

'We had better be going together over the ship, Captain,' said the senior partner; and the three men started to view the perfections of the Nan-Shan from stem to stern, and from her keelson to the trucks of her two stumpy pole-masts.

Captain MacWhirr had begun by taking off his coat, which he hung on the end of a steam windless embodying all the latest improvements.

'My uncle wrote of you favourably by yesterday's mail to our good friends—Messrs. Sigg, you know—and doubtless they'll continue you out there in command,' said the junior partner. 'You'll be able to boast of being in charge of the handiest boat of her size on the coast of China, Captain,' he added.

'Have you? Thank 'ee,' mumbled vaguely MacWhirr, to whom the view of a distant eventuality could appeal no more than the beauty of a wide landscape to a purblind tourist; and his eyes happening at the moment to be at rest upon the lock of the cabin door, he walked up to it, full of purpose, and began to rattle the handle vigorously, while he observed, in his low, earnest voice, 'You can't trust the workmen nowadays. A brand-new lock, and it won't act at all. Stuck fast. See? See?'

As soon as they found themselves alone in their office across the yard: 'You praised that fellow up to Sigg. What is it you see in him?' asked the nephew, with faint contempt.

'I admit he has nothing of your fancy skipper about him, if that's what you mean,' said the elder man, curtly. 'Is the foreman of the joiners on the Nan-Shan outside?...Come in, Bates. How is it that you let Tait's people put us off with a defective lock on the cabin door? The Captain could see directly he set eye on it. Have it replaced at once. The little straws, Bates...the little straws...'

The lock was replaced accordingly, and a few days afterwards the Nan-Shan steamed out to the East, without MacWhirr having offered any further remark as to her fittings, or having been heard to utter a single word hinting at pride in his ship, gratitude for his appointment, or satisfaction at his prospects.

With a temperament neither loquacious nor taciturn he found very little occasion to talk. There were matters of duty, of course—directions, orders, and so on; but the past being to his mind done with, and the future not there yet, the more general actualities of the day required no comment—because facts can speak for themselves with overwhelming precision.

Old Mr Sigg liked a man of few words, and one that 'you could be sure would not try to improve upon his instructions.' MacWhirr satisfying these requirements, was continued in command of the Nan-Shan, and applied himself to the careful navigation of his ship in the China seas. She had come out on a British register, but after some time Messrs. Sigg judged it expedient to transfer her to the Siamese flag.

At the news of the contemplated transfer Jukes grew restless, as if under a sense of personal affront. He went about grumbling to himself, and uttering short scornful laughs. 'Fancy having a ridiculous Noah's Ark elephant in the ensign of one's ship,' he said once at the engine-room door. 'Dash me if I can stand it: I'll throw up the billet. Don't it make you sick, Mr Rout?' The chief engineer only cleared his throat with the air of a man who knows the value of a good billet.

The first morning the new flag floated over the stern of the Nan-Shan Jukes stood looking at it bitterly from the bridge. He struggled with his feelings for a while, and then remarked, 'Queer flag for a man to sail under, sir.'

'What's the matter with the flag?' inquired Captain

MacWhirr. 'Seems all right to me.' And he walked across to the end of the bridge to have a good look.

'Well, it looks queer to me,' burst out Jukes, greatly exasperated, and flung off the bridge.

Captain MacWhirr was amazed at these manners. After a while he stepped quietly into the chart-room, and opened his International Signal Code-book at the plate where the flags of all the nations are correctly figured in gaudy rows. He ran his finger over them, and when he came to Siam he contemplated with great attention the red field and the white elephant. Nothing could be more simple; but to make sure he brought the book out on the bridge for the purpose of comparing the coloured drawing with the real thing at the flagstaff astern. When next Jukes, who was carrying on the duty that day with a sort of suppressed fierceness, happened on the bridge, his commander observed:

'There's nothing amiss with that flag.'

'Isn't there?' mumbled Jukes, falling on his knees before a deck-locker and jerking therefrom viciously a spare lead-line.

'No. I looked up the book. Length twice the breadth and the elephant exactly in the middle. I thought the people ashore would know how to make the local flag. Stands to reason. You were wrong, Jukes...'

'Well, sir,' began Jukes, getting up excitedly, 'all I can say—' He fumbled for the end of the coil of line with trembling hands.

'That's all right.' Captain MacWhirr soothed him, sitting heavily on a little canvas folding-stool he greatly affected. 'All you have to do is to take care they don't hoist the elephant upside-down before they get quite used to it.'

Jukes flung the new lead-line over on the fore-deck with a loud 'Here you are, bo'ss'en—don't forget to wet it thoroughly,' and turned with immense resolution towards his commander; but Captain MacWhirr spread his elbows on the bridge-rail comfortably.

'Because it would be, I suppose, understood as a signal of distress,' he went on. 'What do you think? That elephant there, I take it, stands for something in the nature of the Union Jack in the flag...'

'Does it!' yelled Jukes, so that every head on the Nan-Shan's decks looked towards the bridge. Then he sighed, and with sudden resignation: 'It would certainly be a dam' distressful sight,' he said, meekly.

Later in the day he accosted the chief engineer with a confidential, 'Here, let me tell you the old man's latest.'

Mr Solomon Rout (frequently alluded to as Long Sol, Old Sol, or Father Rout), from finding himself almost invariably the tallest man on board every ship he joined, had acquired the habit of a stooping, leisurely condescension. His hair was scant and sandy, his flat cheeks were pale, his bony wrists and long scholarly hands were pale, too, as though he had lived all his life in the shade.

He smiled from on high at Jukes, and went on smoking and glancing about quietly, in the manner of a kind uncle lending an ear to the tale of an excited schoolboy. Then, greatly amused but impassive, he asked:

'And did you throw up the billet?'

'No,' cried Jukes, raising a weary, discouraged voice above the harsh buzz of the Nan-Shan's friction winches. All of them were hard at work, snatching slings of cargo, high up, to the end of long derricks, only, as it seemed, to let them rip down recklessly by the run. The cargo chains groaned in the gins, clinked on coamings, rattled over the side; and the whole ship quivered, with her long gray flanks smoking in wreaths of steam. 'No,' cried Jukes, 'I didn't. What's the good? I might just as well fling my resignation at this bulkhead. I don't believe you can make a man like that understand anything. He simply knocks me over.'

At that moment Captain MacWhirr, back from the shore, crossed the deck, umbrella in hand, escorted by a mournful, self-possessed Chinaman, walking behind in paper-soled silk shoes, and who also carried an umbrella.

The master of the Nan-Shan, speaking just audibly and gazing at his boots as his manner was, remarked that it would be necessary to call at Fu-chau this trip, and desired Mr Rout to have steam up to-morrow afternoon at one o'clock sharp. He pushed back his hat to wipe his forehead, observing at the same time that he hated going ashore anyhow; while overtopping him, Mr Rout, without deigning a word, smoked austerely, nursing his right elbow in the palm of his left hand. Then Jukes was directed in the same subdued voice to keep the forward 'tween-deck clear of cargo. Two hundred coolies were going to be put down there. The Bun Hin Company were sending that lot home. Twenty-five bags of rice would be coming off in a sampan directly, for stores. All seven-years'-men they were, said Captain MacWhirr, with a camphor-wood chest to every man. The carpenter should be set to work nailing three-inch battens along the deck below, fore and aft, to keep these boxes from shifting in a sea-way. Jukes had better look to it at once. 'D'ye hear, Jukes?' This chinaman here was coming with the ship as far as Fu-chau—a sort of interpreter he would be. Bun Hin's clerk he was, and wanted to have a look at the space. Jukes had better take him forward. 'D'ye hear, Jukes?'

Jukes took care to punctuate these instructions in proper

places with the obligatory 'Yes, sir,' ejaculated without enthusiasm. His brusque 'Come along, John; make look see' set the Chinaman in motion at his heels.

'Wanchee look see, all same look see can do,' said Jukes, who having no talent for foreign languages mangled the very pidgin-English cruelly. He pointed at the open hatch. 'Catchee number one piecie place to sleep in. Eh?'

He was gruff, as became his racial superiority, but not unfriendly. The Chinaman, gazing sad and speechless into the darkness of the hatchway, seemed to stand at the head of a yawning grave.

'No catchee rain down there—savee?' pointed out Jukes. 'Suppose all'ee same fine weather, one piecie coolie-man come topside,' he pursued, warming up imaginatively. 'Make so—Phooooo!' He expanded his chest and blew out his cheeks. 'Savee, John? Breathe—fresh air. Good. Eh? Washee him piecie pants, chow-chow top-side—see, John?'

With his mouth and hands he made exuberant motions of eating rice and washing clothes; and the Chinaman, who concealed his distrust of this pantomime under a collected demeanour tinged by a gentle and refined melancholy, glanced out of his almond eyes from Jukes to the hatch and back again. 'Velly good,' he murmured, in a disconsolate undertone, and hastened smoothly along the decks, dodging obstacles in his course. He disappeared, ducking low under a sling of ten dirty gunny-bags full of some costly merchandise and exhaling a repulsive smell.

Captain MacWhirr meantime had gone on the bridge, and into the chart-room, where a letter, commenced two days before, awaited termination. These long letters began with the words, 'My darling wife,' and the steward, between the scrubbing of the floors and the dusting of chronometer-boxes, snatched at every opportunity to read them. They interested him much more than they possibly could the woman for whose eye they were intended; and this for the reason that they related in minute detail each successive trip of the Nan-Shan.

Her master, faithful to facts, which alone his consciousness reflected, would set them down with painstaking care upon many pages. The house in a northern suburb to which these pages were addressed had a bit of garden before the bow-windows, a deep porch of good appearance, coloured glass with imitation lead frame in the front door. He paid five-and-forty pounds a year for it, and did not think the rent too high, because Mrs MacWhirr (a pretentious person with a scraggy neck and a disdainful manner) was admittedly ladylike, and in the neighbourhood considered as 'quite superior.' The only secret of her life was her abject terror of the time when her husband would come home to stay for good. Under the same roof there dwelt also a daughter called Lydia and a son, Tom. These two were but slightly acquainted with their father. Mainly, they knew him as a rare but privileged visitor, who of an evening smoked his pipe in the dining-room and slept in the house. The lanky girl, upon the whole, was rather ashamed of him; the boy was frankly and utterly indifferent in a straightforward, delightful, unaffected way manly boys have.

And Captain MacWhirr wrote home from the coast of China twelve times every year, desiring quaintly to be 'remembered to the children,' and subscribing himself 'your loving husband,' as calmly as if the words so long used by so many men were, apart from their shape, worn-out things, and of a faded meaning.

The China seas north and south are narrow seas. They are seas full of every-day, eloquent facts, such as islands, sand-banks, reefs, swift and changeable currents—tangled facts that nevertheless speak to a seaman in clear and definite language. Their speech appealed to Captain MacWhirr's sense of realities so forcibly that he had given up his state-room below and practically lived all his days on the bridge of his ship, often having his meals sent up, and sleeping at night in the chart-room. And he indited there his home letters. Each of them, without exception, contained the phrase, 'The weather has been very fine this trip,' or some other form of a statement to that effect. And this statement, too, in its wonderful persistence, was of the same perfect accuracy as all the others they contained.

Mr Rout likewise wrote letters; only no one on board knew how chatty he could be pen in hand, because the chief engineer had enough imagination to keep his desk locked. His wife relished his style greatly. They were a childless couple, and Mrs Rout, a big, high-bosomed, jolly woman of forty, shared with Mr Rout's toothless and venerable mother a little cottage near Teddington. She would run over her correspondence, at breakfast, with lively eyes, and scream out interesting passages in a joyous voice at the deaf old lady, prefacing each extract by the warning shout, 'Solomon says!' She had the trick of firing off Solomon's utterances also upon strangers, astonishing them easily by the unfamiliar text and the unexpectedly jocular vein of these quotations. On the day the new curate called for the first time at the cottage, she found occasion to remark, 'As Solomon says: 'the engineers that go down to the sea in ships behold the wonders of sailor nature';' when a change in the visitor's countenance made her stop and stare.

'Solomon...Oh!...Mrs Rout,' stuttered the young man, very red in the face, 'I must say...I don't...'

'He's my husband,' she announced in a great shout, throwing

herself back in the chair. Perceiving the joke, she laughed immoderately with a handkerchief to her eyes, while he sat wearing a forced smile, and, from his inexperience of jolly women, fully persuaded that she must be deplorably insane. They were excellent friends afterwards; for, absolving her from irreverent intention, he came to think she was a very worthy person indeed; and he learned in time to receive without flinching other scraps of Solomon's wisdom.

'For my part,' Solomon was reported by his wife to have said once, 'give me the dullest ass for a skipper before a rogue. There is a way to take a fool; but a rogue is smart and slippery.' This was an airy generalization drawn from the particular case of Captain MacWhirr's honesty, which, in itself, had the heavy obviousness of a lump of clay. On the other hand, Mr Jukes, unable to generalize, unmarried, and unengaged, was in the habit of opening his heart after another fashion to an old chum and former shipmate, actually serving as second officer on board an Atlantic liner.

First of all he would insist upon the advantages of the Eastern trade, hinting at its superiority to the Western ocean service. He extolled the sky, the seas, the ships, and the easy life of the Far East. The Nan-Shan, he affirmed, was second to none as a sea-boat.

'We have no brass-bound uniforms, but then we are like brothers here,' he wrote. 'We all mess together and live like fighting-cocks...All the chaps of the black-squad are as decent as they make that kind, and old Sol, the Chief, is a dry stick. We are good friends. As to our old man, you could not find a quieter skipper. Sometimes you would think he hadn't sense enough to see anything wrong. And yet it isn't that. Can't be. He has been in command for a good few years now. He doesn't do anything actually foolish, and gets his ship along all right without worrying anybody. I believe he hasn't brains enough to enjoy kicking up a row. I don't take advantage of him. I would scorn it. Outside the routine of duty he doesn't seem to understand more than half of what you tell him. We get a laugh out of this at times; but it is dull, too, to be with a man like this—in the long-run. Old Sol says he hasn't much conversation. Conversation! O Lord! He never talks. The other day I had been yarning under the bridge with one of the engineers, and he must have heard us. When I came up to take my watch, he steps out of the chart-room and has a good look all round, peeps over at the sidelights, glances at the compass, squints upward at the stars. That's his regular performance. By-and-by he says: 'Was that you talking just now in the port alleyway?' 'Yes, sir.' 'With the third engineer?' 'Yes, sir.' He walks off to starboard, and sits under the dodger on a little campstool of his, and for half an hour perhaps he makes no sound, except that I heard him sneeze once. Then after a while I hear him getting up over there, and he strolls across to port, where I was. 'I can't understand what you can find to talk about,' says he. 'Two solid hours. I am not blaming you. I see people ashore at it all day long, and then in the evening they sit down and keep at it over the drinks. Must be saying the same things over and over again. I can't understand.'

'Did you ever hear anything like that? And he was so patient about it. It made me quite sorry for him. But he is exasperating, too, sometimes. Of course one would not do anything to vex him even if it were worth while. But it isn't. He's so jolly innocent that if you were to put your thumb to your nose and wave your fingers at him he would only wonder gravely to himself what got into you. He told me once quite simply that he found it very difficult to make out what made people always act so queerly. He's too dense to trouble about, and that's the truth.'

Thus wrote Mr Jukes to his chum in the Western ocean trade, out of the fullness of his heart and the liveliness of his fancy.

He had expressed his honest opinion. It was not worthwhile trying to impress a man of that sort. If the world had been full of such men, life would have probably appeared to Jukes an unentertaining and unprofitable business. He was not alone in his opinion. The sea itself, as if sharing Mr Jukes' good-natured forbearance, had never put itself out to startle the silent man, who seldom looked up, and wandered innocently over the waters with the only visible purpose of getting food, raiment, and house-room for three people ashore. Dirty weather he had known, of course. He had been made wet, uncomfortable, tired in the usual way, felt at the time and presently forgotten. So that upon the whole he had been justified in reporting fine weather at home. But he had never been given a glimpse of immeasurable strength and of immoderate wrath, the wrath that passes exhausted but never appeased—the wrath and fury of the passionate sea. He knew it existed, as we know that crime and abominations exist; he had heard of it as a peaceable citizen in a town hears of battles, famines and floods, and yet knows nothing of what these things mean—though, indeed, he may have been mixed up in a street row, have gone without his dinner once, or been soaked to the skin in a shower. Captain MacWhirr had sailed over the surface of the oceans as some men go skimming over the years of existence to sink gently into a placid grave, ignorant of life to the last, without ever having been made to see all it may contain of perfidy, of violence and of terror. There are on sea and land such men thus fortunate—or thus disdained by destiny or by the sea.

II

Observing the steady fall of the barometer, Captain MacWhirr thought, 'There's some dirty weather knocking about.' This is precisely what he thought. He had had an experience of moderately dirty weather—the term dirty as applied to the weather implying only moderate discomfort to the seaman. Had he been informed by an indisputable authority that the end of the world was to be finally accomplished by a catastrophic disturbance of the atmosphere, he would have assimilated the information under the simple idea of dirty weather, and no other, because he had no experience of cataclysms, and belief does not necessarily imply comprehension. The wisdom of his county had pronounced by means of an Act of Parliament that before he could be considered as fit to take charge of a ship he should be able to answer certain simple questions on the subject of circular storms such as hurricanes, cyclones, typhoons; and apparently he had answered them, since he was now in command of the Nan-Shan in the China seas during the season of typhoons. But if he had answered he remembered nothing of it. He was, however, conscious of being made uncomfortable by the clammy heat. He came out on the bridge, and found no relief to this oppression. The air seemed thick. He gasped like a fish, and began to believe himself greatly out of sorts.

The Nan-Shan was ploughing a vanishing furrow upon the circle of the sea that had the surface and the shimmer of an undulating piece of gray silk. The sun, pale and without rays, poured down leaden heat in a strangely indecisive light, and the Chinamen were lying prostrate about the decks. Their bloodless, pinched, yellow faces were like the faces of bilious invalids. Captain MacWhirr noticed two of them especially, stretched out on their backs below the bridge. As soon as they had closed their eyes they seemed dead. Three others, however, were quarrelling barbarously away forward; and one big fellow, half naked, with herculean shoulders, was hanging limply over a winch; another, sitting on the deck, his knees up and his head drooping sideways in a girlish attitude, was plaiting his pigtail with infinite languor depicted in his whole person and in the very movement of his fingers. The smoke struggled with difficulty out of the funnel, and instead of streaming away spread itself out like an infernal sort of cloud, smelling of sulphur and raining soot all over the decks.

'What the devil are you doing there, Mr Jukes?' asked Captain MacWhirr.

This unusual form of address, though mumbled rather than spoken, caused the body of Mr Jukes to start as though it had been prodded under the fifth rib. He had had a low bench brought on the bridge, and sitting on it, with a length of rope curled about his feet and a piece of canvas stretched over his knees, was pushing a sail-needle vigorously. He looked up, and his surprise gave to his eyes an expression of innocence and candour.

'I am only roping some of that new set of bags we made last trip for whipping up coals,' he remonstrated, gently. 'We shall want them for the next coaling, sir.'

'What became of the others?'

'Why, worn out of course, sir.'

Captain MacWhirr, after glaring down irresolutely at his chief mate, disclosed the gloomy and cynical conviction that more than half of them had been lost overboard, 'if only the truth was known,' and retired to the other end of the bridge. Jukes, exasperated by this unprovoked attack, broke the needle at the second stitch, and dropping his work got up and cursed the heat in a violent undertone.

The propeller thumped, the three Chinamen forward had given up squabbling very suddenly, and the one who had been plaiting his tail clasped his legs and stared dejectedly over his knees. The lurid sunshine cast faint and sickly shadows. The swell ran higher and swifter every moment, and the ship lurched heavily in the smooth, deep hollows of the sea.

'I wonder where that beastly swell comes from,' said Jukes aloud, recovering himself after a stagger.

'North-east,' grunted the literal MacWhirr, from his side of the bridge. 'There's some dirty weather knocking about. Go and look at the glass.'

When Jukes came out of the chart-room, the cast of his countenance had changed to thoughtfulness and concern. He caught hold of the bridge-rail and stared ahead.

The temperature in the engine-room had gone up to a hundred and seventeen degrees. Irritated voices were ascending through the skylight and through the fiddle of the stokehold in a harsh and resonant uproar, mingled with angry clangs and scrapes of metal, as if men with limbs of iron and throats of bronze had been quarrelling down there. The second engineer was falling foul of the stokers for letting the steam go down. He was a man with arms like a blacksmith, and generally feared; but that afternoon the stokers were answering him back recklessly, and slammed the furnace doors with the fury of despair. Then the noise ceased suddenly, and the second engineer appeared, emerging out of the stokehold streaked with grime and soaking wet like a chimney-sweep coming out of a well. As soon as his head was clear of the fiddle he began to scold Jukes for not trimming properly the stokehold ventilators; and in answer Jukes made with his hands deprecatory soothing signs meaning: 'No wind—can't be helped—you can see for yourself.' But the other wouldn't hear reason. His teeth flashed angrily in his dirty face. He didn't mind, he said, the trouble of punching their blanked heads down there, blank his soul, but did the condemned sailors think you could keep steam up in the God-forsaken boilers simply by knocking the blanked stokers about? No, by George! You had to get some draught, too—may he be everlastingly blanked for a swab-headed deck-hand if you didn't! And the chief, too, rampaging before the steam-gauge and carrying on like a lunatic up and down the engine-room ever since noon. What did Jukes think he was stuck up there for, if he couldn't get one of his decayed, good-for-nothing deck-cripples to turn the ventilators to the wind?

The relations of the 'engine-room' and the 'deck' of the Nan-Shan were, as is known, of a brotherly nature; therefore Jukes leaned over and begged the other in a restrained tone not to make a disgusting ass of himself; the skipper was on the other side of the bridge. But the second declared mutinously that he didn't care a rap who was on the other side of the bridge, and Jukes, passing in a flash from lofty disapproval into a state of exaltation, invited him in unflattering terms to come up and twist the beastly things to please himself, and catch such wind as a donkey of his sort could find. The second rushed up to the fray. He flung himself at the port ventilator as though he meant to tear it out bodily and toss it overboard. All he did was to move the cowl round a few inches, with an enormous expenditure of force, and seemed spent in the effort. He leaned against the back of the wheelhouse, and Jukes walked up to him.

'Oh, Heavens!' ejaculated the engineer in a feeble voice. He lifted his eyes to the sky, and then let his glassy stare descend to meet the horizon that, tilting up to an angle of forty degrees, seemed to hang on a slant for a while and settled down slowly. 'Heavens! Phew! What's up, anyhow?'

Jukes, straddling his long legs like a pair of compasses, put on an air of superiority. 'We're going to catch it this time,' he said. 'The barometer is tumbling down like anything, Harry. And you trying to kick up that silly row…'

The word 'barometer' seemed to revive the second engineer's mad animosity. Collecting afresh all his energies, he directed Jukes in a low and brutal tone to shove the unmentionable instrument down his gory throat. Who cared for his crimson barometer? It was the steam—the steam—that was going down; and what between the firemen going faint and the chief going silly, it was worse than a dog's life for him; he didn't care a tinker's curse how soon the whole show was blown out of the water. He seemed on the point of having a cry, but after regaining his breath he muttered darkly, 'I'll faint them,' and dashed off. He stopped upon the fiddle long enough to shake his fist at the unnatural daylight, and dropped into the dark hole with a whoop.

When Jukes turned, his eyes fell upon the rounded back and the big red ears of Captain MacWhirr, who had come across. He did not look at his chief officer, but said at once, 'That's a very violent man, that second engineer.'

'Jolly good second, anyhow,' grunted Jukes. 'They can't keep up steam,' he added, rapidly, and made a grab at the rail against the coming lurch.

Captain MacWhirr, unprepared, took a run and brought himself up with a jerk by an awning stanchion.

'A profane man,' he said, obstinately. 'If this goes on, I'll have to get rid of him the first chance.'

'It's the heat,' said Jukes. 'The weather's awful. It would

make a saint swear. Even up here I feel exactly as if I had my head tied up in a woollen blanket.'

Captain MacWhirr looked up. 'D'ye mean to say, Mr Jukes, you ever had your head tied up in a blanket? What was that for?'

'It's a manner of speaking, sir,' said Jukes, stolidly.

'Some of you fellows do go on! What's that about saints swearing? I wish you wouldn't talk so wild. What sort of saint would that be that would swear? No more saint than yourself, I expect. And what's a blanket got to do with it—or the weather either...The heat does not make me swear—does it? It's filthy bad temper. That's what it is. And what's the good of your talking like this?'

Thus Captain MacWhirr expostulated against the use of images in speech, and at the end electrified Jukes by a contemptuous snort, followed by words of passion and resentment: 'Damme! I'll fire him out of the ship if he don't look out.'

And Jukes, incorrigible, thought: 'Goodness me! Somebody's put a new inside to my old man. Here's temper, if you like. Of course it's the weather; what else? It would make an angel quarrelsome—let alone a saint.'

All the Chinamen on deck appeared at their last gasp.

At its setting the sun had a diminished diameter and an expiring brown, rayless glow, as if millions of centuries elapsing since the morning had brought it near its end. A dense bank of cloud became visible to the northward; it had a sinister dark olive tint, and lay low and motionless upon the sea, resembling a solid obstacle in the path of the ship. She went floundering towards it like an exhausted creature driven to its death. The coppery twilight retired slowly, and the darkness brought out overhead a swarm of unsteady, big stars, that, as if blown upon, flickered exceedingly and seemed to hang very near the earth. At eight o'clock Jukes went into the chart-room to write up the ship's log.

He copies neatly out of the rough-book the number of miles, the course of the ship, and in the column for 'wind' scrawled the word 'calm' from top to bottom of the eight hours since noon. He was exasperated by the continuous, monotonous rolling of the ship. The heavy inkstand would slide away in a manner that suggested perverse intelligence in dodging the pen. Having written in the large space under the head of 'Remarks' 'Heat very oppressive,' he stuck the end of the penholder in his teeth, pipe fashion, and mopped his face carefully.

'Ship rolling heavily in a high cross swell,' he began again, and commented to himself, 'Heavily is no word for it.' Then he wrote: 'Sunset threatening, with a low bank of clouds to N. and E. Sky clear overhead.'

Sprawling over the table with arrested pen, he glanced out of the door, and in that frame of his vision he saw all the stars flying upwards between the teakwood jambs on a black sky. The whole lot took flight together and disappeared, leaving only a blackness flecked with white flashes, for the sea was as black as the sky and speckled with foam afar. The stars that had flown to the roll came back on the return swing of the ship, rushing downwards in their glittering multitude, not of fiery points, but enlarged to tiny discs brilliant with a clear wet sheen.

Jukes watched the flying big stars for a moment, and then wrote: '8 p.m. Swell increasing. Ship labouring and taking water on her decks. Battened down the coolies for the night. Barometer still falling.' He paused, and thought to himself, 'Perhaps nothing whatever'll come of it.' And then he closed resolutely his entries: 'Every appearance of a typhoon coming on.'

On going out he had to stand aside, and Captain MacWhirr strode over the doorstep without saying a word or making a sign.

'Shut the door, Mr Jukes, will you?' he cried from within.

Jukes turned back to do so, muttering ironically: 'Afraid to catch cold, I suppose.' It was his watch below, but he yearned for communion with his kind; and he remarked cheerily to the second mate: 'Doesn't look so bad, after all—does it?'

The second mate was marching to and fro on the bridge, tripping down with small steps one moment, and the next climbing with difficulty the shifting slope of the deck. At the sound of Jukes' voice he stood still, facing forward, but made no reply.

'Hallo! That's a heavy one,' said Jukes, swaying to meet the long roll till his lowered hand touched the planks. This time the second mate made in his throat a noise of an unfriendly nature.

He was an oldish, shabby little fellow, with bad teeth and no hair on his face. He had been shipped in a hurry in Shanghai, that trip when the second officer brought from home had delayed the ship three hours in port by contriving (in some manner Captain MacWhirr could never understand) to fall overboard into an empty coal-lighter lying alongside, and had to be sent ashore to the hospital with concussion of the brain and a broken limb or two.

Jukes was not discouraged by the unsympathetic sound. 'The Chinamen must be having a lovely time of it down there,' he said. 'It's lucky for them the old girl has the easiest roll of any ship I've ever been in. There now! This one wasn't so bad.'

'You wait,' snarled the second mate.

With his sharp nose, red at the tip, and his thin pinched lips, he always looked as though he were raging inwardly; and he was concise in his speech to the point of rudeness. All his time off duty he spent in his cabin with the door shut, keeping so still in there that he was supposed to fall asleep as soon as he had disappeared; but the man who came in to wake him for his watch on deck would invariably find him with his eyes wide open, flat on his back in the bunk, and glaring irritably from a soiled pillow. He never wrote any letters, did not seem to hope for news from anywhere; and though he had been heard once to mention West Hartlepool, it was with extreme bitterness, and only in connection with the extortionate charges of a boarding-house. He was one of those men who are picked up at need in the ports of the world. They are competent enough, appear hopelessly hard up, show no evidence of any sort of vice, and carry about them all the signs of manifest failure. They come aboard on an emergency, care for no ship afloat, live in their own atmosphere of casual connection amongst their shipmates who know nothing of them, and make up their minds to leave at inconvenient times. They clear out with no words of leavetaking in some God-forsaken port other men would fear to be stranded in, and go ashore in company of a shabby sea-chest, corded like a treasure-box, and with an air of shaking the ship's dust off their feet.

'You wait,' he repeated, balanced in great swings with his back to Jukes, motionless and implacable.

'Do you mean to say we are going to catch it hot?' asked Jukes with boyish interest.

'Say?...I say nothing. You don't catch me,' snapped the little second mate, with a mixture of pride, scorn, and cunning, as if Jukes' question had been a trap cleverly detected. 'Oh, no! None of you here shall make a fool of me if I know it,' he mumbled to himself.

Jukes reflected rapidly that this second mate was a mean

little beast, and in his heart he wished poor Jack Allen had never smashed himself up in the coal-lighter. The far-off blackness ahead of the ship was like another night seen through the starry night of the earth—the starless night of the immensities beyond the created universe, revealed in its appalling stillness through a low fissure in the glittering sphere of which the earth is the kernel.

'Whatever there might be about,' said Jukes, 'we are steaming straight into it.'

'You've said it,' caught up the second mate, always with his back to Jukes. 'You've said it, mind—not I.'

'Oh, go to Jericho!' said Jukes, frankly; and the other emitted a triumphant little chuckle.

'You've said it,' he repeated.

'And what of that?'

'I've known some real good men get into trouble with their skippers for saying a dam' sight less,' answered the second mate feverishly. 'Oh, no! You don't catch me.'

'You seem deucedly anxious not to give yourself away,' said Jukes, completely soured by such absurdity. 'I wouldn't be afraid to say what I think.'

'Aye, to me! That's no great trick. I am nobody, and well I know it.'

The ship, after a pause of comparative steadiness, started upon a series of rolls, one worse than the other, and for a time Jukes, preserving his equilibrium, was too busy to open his mouth. As soon as the violent swinging had quieted down somewhat, he said: 'This is a bit too much of a good thing. Whether anything is coming or not I think she ought to be put head on to that swell. The old man is just gone in to lie down. Hang me if I don't speak to him.'

But when he opened the door of the chart-room he saw his captain reading a book. Captain MacWhirr was not lying down: he was standing up with one hand grasping the edge of the bookshelf and the other holding open before his face a thick volume. The lamp wriggled in the gimbals, the loosened books toppled from side to side on the shelf, the long barometer swung in jerky circles, the table altered its slant every moment. In the midst of all this stir and movement Captain MacWhirr, holding on, showed his eyes above the upper edge, and asked, 'What's the matter?'

'Swell getting worse, sir.'

'Noticed that in here,' muttered Captain MacWhirr. 'Anything wrong?'

Jukes, inwardly disconcerted by the seriousness of the eyes looking at him over the top of the book, produced an embarrassed grin.

'Rolling like old boots,' he said, sheepishly.

'Aye! Very heavy—very heavy. What do you want?'

At this Jukes lost his footing and began to flounder. 'I was thinking of our passengers,' he said, in the manner of a man clutching at a straw.

'Passengers?' wondered the Captain, gravely. 'What passengers?'

'Why, the Chinamen, sir,' explained Jukes, very sick of this conversation.

'The Chinamen! Why don't you speak plainly? Couldn't tell what you meant. Never heard a lot of coolies spoken of as passengers before. Passengers, indeed! What's come to you?'

Captain MacWhirr, closing the book on his forefinger, lowered his arm and looked completely mystified. 'Why are you thinking of the Chinamen, Mr Jukes?' he inquired.

Jukes took a plunge, like a man driven to it. 'She's rolling her decks full of water, sir. Thought you might put her head on perhaps—for a while. Till this goes down a bit—very soon, I dare say. Head to the eastward. I never knew a ship roll like this.'

He held on in the doorway, and Captain MacWhirr, feeling his grip on the shelf inadequate, made up his mind to let go in a hurry, and fell heavily on the couch.

'Head to the eastward?' he said, struggling to sit up. 'That's more than four points off her course.'

'Yes, sir. Fifty degrees... Would just bring her head far enough round to meet this...'

Captain MacWhirr was now sitting up. He had not dropped the book, and he had not lost his place.

'To the eastward?' he repeated, with dawning astonishment. 'To the... Where do you think we are bound to? You want me to haul a full-powered steamship four points off her course to make the Chinamen comfortable! Now, I've heard more than enough of mad things done in the world—but this... If I didn't know you, Jukes, I would think you were in liquor. Steer four points off... And what afterwards? Steer four points over the other way, I suppose, to make the course good. What put it into your head that I would start to tack a steamer as if she were a sailing-ship?'

'Jolly good thing she isn't,' threw in Jukes, with bitter readiness. 'She would have rolled every blessed stick out of her this afternoon.'

'Aye! And you just would have had to stand and see them go,' said Captain MacWhirr, showing a certain animation. 'It's a dead calm, isn't it?'

'It is, sir. But there's something out of the common coming, for sure.'

'Maybe. I suppose you have a notion I should be getting out of the way of that dirt,' said Captain MacWhirr, speaking with the utmost simplicity of manner and tone, and fixing the oilcloth on the floor with a heavy stare. Thus he noticed neither Jukes' discomfiture nor the mixture of vexation and astonished respect on his face.

'Now, here's this book,' he continued with deliberation, slapping his thigh with the closed volume. 'I've been reading the chapter on the storms there.'

This was true. He had been reading the chapter on the storms. When he had entered the chart-room, it was with no intention of taking the book down. Some influence in the air—the same influence, probably, that caused the steward to bring without orders the Captain's sea-boots and oilskin coat up to the chart-room—had as it were guided his hand to the shelf; and without taking the time to sit down he had waded with a conscious effort into the terminology of the subject. He lost himself amongst advancing semi-circles, left- and right-hand quadrants, the curves of the tracks, the probable bearing of the centre, the shifts of wind and the readings of barometer. He tried to bring all these things into a definite relation to himself, and ended by becoming contemptuously angry with such a lot of words, and with so much advice, all head-work and supposition, without a glimmer of certitude.

'It's the damnedest thing, Jukes,' he said. 'If a fellow was to believe all that's in there, he would be running most of his time all over the sea trying to get behind the weather.'

Again he slapped his leg with the book; and Jukes opened his mouth, but said nothing.

'Running to get behind the weather! Do you understand that, Mr Jukes? It's the maddest thing!' ejaculated Captain

MacWhirr, with pauses, gazing at the floor profoundly. 'You would think an old woman had been writing this. It passes me. If that thing means anything useful, then it means that I should at once alter the course away, away to the devil somewhere, and come booming down on Fu-chau from the northward at the tail of this dirty weather that's supposed to be knocking about in our way. From the north! Do you understand, Mr Jukes? Three hundred extra miles to the distance, and a pretty coal bill to show. I couldn't bring myself to do that if every word in there was gospel truth, Mr Jukes. Don't you expect me...'

And Jukes, silent, marvelled at this display of feeling and loquacity.

'But the truth is that you don't know if the fellow is right, anyhow. How can you tell what a gale is made of till you get it? He isn't aboard here, is he? Very well. Here he says that the centre of them things bears eight points off the wind; but we haven't got any wind, for all the barometer falling. Where's his centre now?'

'We will get the wind presently,' mumbled Jukes.

'Let it come, then,' said Captain MacWhirr, with dignified indignation. 'It's only to let you see, Mr Jukes, that you don't find everything in books. All these rules for dodging breezes and circumventing the winds of heaven, Mr Jukes, seem to me the maddest thing, when you come to look at it sensibly.'

He raised his eyes, saw Jukes gazing at him dubiously, and tried to illustrate his meaning.

'About as queer as your extraordinary notion of dodging the ship head to sea, for I don't know how long, to make the Chinamen comfortable; whereas all we've got to do is to take them to Fu-chau, being timed to get there before noon on Friday. If the weather delays me—very well. There's your log-book to talk straight about the weather. But suppose I went swinging off my course and came in two days late, and they asked me: 'Where have you been all that time, Captain?' What could I say to that? 'Went around to dodge the bad weather,' I would say. 'It must've been dam' bad,' they would say. 'Don't know,' I would have to say; 'I've dodged clear of it.' See that, Jukes? I have been thinking it all out this afternoon.'

He looked up again in his unseeing, unimaginative way. No one had ever heard him say so much at one time. Jukes, with his arms open in the doorway, was like a man invited to behold a miracle. Unbounded wonder was the intellectual meaning of his eye, while incredulity was seated in his whole countenance.

'A gale is a gale, Mr Jukes,' resumed the Captain, 'and a full-powered steam-ship has got to face it. There's just so much dirty weather knocking about the world, and the proper thing is to go through it with none of what old Captain Wilson of the Melita calls 'storm strategy.' The other day ashore I heard him hold forth about it to a lot of shipmasters who came in and sat at a table next to mine. It seemed to me the greatest nonsense. He was telling them how he outmanoeuvred, I think he said, a terrific gale, so that it never came nearer than fifty miles to him. A neat piece of head-work he called it. How he knew there was a terrific gale fifty miles off beats me altogether. It was like listening to a crazy man. I would have thought Captain Wilson was old enough to know better.'

Captain MacWhirr ceased for a moment, then said, 'It's your watch below, Mr Jukes?'

Jukes came to himself with a start. 'Yes, sir.'

'Leave orders to call me at the slightest change,' said the Captain. He reached up to put the book away, and tucked his legs upon the couch. 'Shut the door so that it don't fly open, will you? I can't stand a door banging. They've put a lot of rubbishy locks into this ship, I must say.'

Captain MacWhirr closed his eyes.

He did so to rest himself. He was tired, and he experienced that state of mental vacuity which comes at the end of an exhaustive discussion that has liberated some belief matured in the course of meditative years. He had indeed been making his confession of faith, had he only known it; and its effect was to make Jukes, on the other side of the door, stand scratching his head for a good while.

Captain MacWhirr opened his eyes.

He thought he must have been asleep. What was that loud noise? Wind? Why had he not been called? The lamp wriggled in its gimbals, the barometer swung in circles, the table altered its slant every moment; a pair of limp sea-boots with collapsed tops went sliding past the couch. He put out his hand instantly, and captured one.

Jukes' face appeared in a crack of the door: only his face, very red, with staring eyes. The flame of the lamp leaped, a piece of paper flew up, a rush of air enveloped Captain MacWhirr. Beginning to draw on the boot, he directed an expectant gaze at Jukes' swollen, excited features.

'Came on like this,' shouted Jukes, 'five minutes ago…all of a sudden.'

The head disappeared with a bang, and a heavy splash and patter of drops swept past the closed door as if a pailful of melted lead had been flung against the house. A whistling could be heard now upon the deep vibrating noise outside. The stuffy chart-room seemed as full of draughts as a shed. Captain MacWhirr collared the other sea-boot on its violent passage along the floor. He was not flustered, but he could not find at once the opening for inserting his foot. The shoes he had flung off were scurrying from end to end of the cabin, gambolling playfully over each other like puppies. As soon as he stood up he kicked at them viciously, but without effect.

He threw himself into the attitude of a lunging fencer, to reach after his oilskin coat; and afterwards he staggered all over the confined space while he jerked himself into it. Very grave, straddling his legs far apart, and stretching his neck, he started to tie deliberately the strings of his sou'-wester under his chin, with thick fingers that trembled slightly. He went through all the movements of a woman putting on her bonnet before a glass, with a strained, listening attention, as though he had expected every moment to hear the shout of his name in the confused clamour that had suddenly beset his ship. Its increase filled his ears while he was getting ready to go out and confront whatever it might mean. It was tumultuous and very loud—made up of the rush of the wind, the crashes of the sea, with that prolonged deep vibration of the air, like the roll of an immense and remote drum beating the charge of the gale.

He stood for a moment in the light of the lamp, thick, clumsy, shapeless in his panoply of combat, vigilant and red-faced.

'There's a lot of weight in this,' he muttered.

As soon as he attempted to open the door the wind caught it. Clinging to the handle, he was dragged out over the doorstep, and at once found himself engaged with the wind in a sort of personal scuffle whose object was the shutting of that door. At the last moment a tongue of air scurried in and licked out the flame of the lamp.

Ahead of the ship he perceived a great darkness lying upon a multitude of white flashes; on the starboard beam a few amazing stars drooped, dim and fitful, above an immense waste of broken seas, as if seen through a mad drift of smoke.

On the bridge a knot of men, indistinct and toiling, were making great efforts in the light of the wheelhouse windows that shone mistily on their heads and backs. Suddenly darkness closed upon one pane, then on another. The voices of the lost group reached him after the manner of men's voices in a gale, in shreds and fragments of forlorn shouting snatched past the ear. All at once Jukes appeared at his side, yelling, with his head down.

'Watch—put in—wheelhouse shutters—glass—afraid—blow in.'

Jukes heard his commander upbraiding.

'This—come—anything—warning—call me.'

He tried to explain, with the uproar pressing on his lips.

'Light air—remained—bridge—sudden—north-east—could turn—thought—you—sure—hear.'

They had gained the shelter of the weather-cloth, and could converse with raised voices, as people quarrel.

'I got the hands along to cover up all the ventilators. Good job I had remained on deck. I didn't think you would be asleep, and so…What did you say, sir? What?'

'Nothing,' cried Captain MacWhirr. 'I said—all right.'

'By all the powers! We've got it this time,' observed Jukes in a howl.

'You haven't altered her course?' inquired Captain MacWhirr, straining his voice.

'No, sir. Certainly not. Wind came out right ahead. And here comes the head sea.'

A plunge of the ship ended in a shock as if she had landed her forefoot upon something solid. After a moment of stillness a lofty flight of sprays drove hard with the wind upon their faces.

'Keep her at it as long as we can,' shouted Captain MacWhirr.

Before Jukes had squeezed the salt water out of his eyes all the stars had disappeared.

III

Jukes was as ready a man as any half-dozen young mates that may be caught by casting a net upon the waters; and though he had been somewhat taken aback by the startling viciousness of the first squall, he had pulled himself together on the instant, had called out the hands and had rushed them along to secure such openings about the deck as had not been already battened down earlier in the evening. Shouting in his fresh, stentorian voice, 'Jump, boys, and bear a hand!' he led in the work, telling himself the while that he had 'just expected this.'

But at the same time he was growing aware that this was rather more than he had expected. From the first stir of the air felt on his cheek the gale seemed to take upon itself the accumulated impetus of an avalanche. Heavy sprays enveloped the Nan-Shan from stem to stern, and instantly in the midst of her regular rolling she began to jerk and plunge as though she had gone mad with fright.

Jukes thought, 'This is no joke.' While he was exchanging explanatory yells with his captain, a sudden lowering of the darkness came upon the night, falling before their vision like something palpable. It was as if the masked lights of the world had been turned down. Jukes was uncritically glad to have his captain at hand. It relieved him as though that man had, by simply coming on deck, taken most of the gale's weight upon his shoulders. Such is the prestige, the privilege, and the burden of command.

Captain MacWhirr could expect no relief of that sort from any one on earth. Such is the loneliness of command. He was trying to see, with that watchful manner of a seaman who stares into the wind's eye as if into the eye of an adversary, to penetrate the hidden intention and guess the aim and force of the thrust. The strong wind swept at him out of a vast obscurity; he felt under his feet the uneasiness of his ship, and he could not even discern the shadow of her shape. He wished it were not so; and very still he waited, feeling stricken by a blind man's helplessness.

To be silent was natural to him, dark or shine. Jukes, at his elbow, made himself heard yelling cheerily in the gusts, 'We must have got the worst of it at once, sir.' A faint burst of lightning quivered all round, as if flashed into a cavern—into a black and secret chamber of the sea, with a floor of foaming crests.

It unveiled for a sinister, fluttering moment a ragged mass of clouds hanging low, the lurch of the long outlines of the ship, the black figures of men caught on the bridge, heads forward, as if petrified in the act of butting. The darkness palpitated down upon all this, and then the real thing came at last.

It was something formidable and swift, like the sudden smashing of a vial of wrath. It seemed to explode all round the ship with an overpowering concussion and a rush of great waters, as if an immense dam had been blown up to windward. In an instant the men lost touch of each other. This is the disintegrating power of a great wind: it isolates one from one's kind. An earthquake, a landslip, an avalanche, overtake a man incidentally, as it were—without passion. A furious gale attacks him like a personal enemy, tries to grasp his limbs, fastens upon his mind, seeks to rout his very spirit out of him.

Jukes was driven away from his commander. He fancied

himself whirled a great distance through the air. Everything disappeared—even, for a moment, his power of thinking; but his hand had found one of the rail-stanchions. His distress was by no means alleviated by an inclination to disbelieve the reality of this experience. Though young, he had seen some bad weather, and had never doubted his ability to imagine the worst; but this was so much beyond his powers of fancy that it appeared incompatible with the existence of any ship whatever. He would have been incredulous about himself in the same way, perhaps, had he not been so harassed by the necessity of exerting a wrestling effort against a force trying to tear him away from his hold. Moreover, the conviction of not being utterly destroyed returned to him through the sensations of being half-drowned, bestially shaken, and partly choked.

It seemed to him he remained there precariously alone with the stanchion for a long, long time. The rain poured on him, flowed, drove in sheets. He breathed in gasps; and sometimes the water he swallowed was fresh and sometimes it was salt. For the most part he kept his eyes shut tight, as if suspecting his sight might be destroyed in the immense flurry of the elements. When he ventured to blink hastily, he derived some moral support from the green gleam of the starboard light shining feebly upon the flight of rain and sprays. He was actually looking at it when its ray fell upon the uprearing sea which put it out. He saw the head of the wave topple over, adding the mite of its crash to the tremendous uproar raging around him, and almost at the same instant the stanchion was wrenched away from his embracing arms. After a crushing thump on his back he found himself suddenly afloat and borne upwards. His first irresistible notion was that the whole China Sea had climbed on the bridge. Then, more sanely, he concluded himself gone overboard. All the time he was being tossed, flung, and rolled in great volumes of water, he kept on repeating mentally, with the utmost precipitation, the words: 'My God! My God! My God! My God!'

All at once, in a revolt of misery and despair, he formed the crazy resolution to get out of that. And he began to thresh about with his arms and legs. But as soon as he commenced his wretched struggles he discovered that he had become somehow mixed up with a face, an oilskin coat, somebody's boots. He clawed ferociously all these things in turn, lost them, found them again, lost them once more, and finally was himself caught in the firm clasp of a pair of stout arms. He returned the embrace closely round a thick solid body. He had found his captain.

They tumbled over and over, tightening their hug. Suddenly the water let them down with a brutal bang; and, stranded against the side of the wheelhouse, out of breath and bruised, they were left to stagger up in the wind and hold on where they could.

Jukes came out of it rather horrified, as though he had escaped some unparalleled outrage directed at his feelings. It weakened his faith in himself. He started shouting aimlessly to the man he could feel near him in that fiendish blackness, 'Is it you, sir? Is it you, sir?' till his temples seemed ready to burst. And he heard in answer a voice, as if crying far away, as if screaming to him fretfully from a very great distance, the one word 'Yes!' Other seas swept again over the bridge. He received them defencelessly right over his bare head, with both his hands engaged in holding.

The motion of the ship was extravagant. Her lurches had an appalling helplessness: she pitched as if taking a header into a void, and seemed to find a wall to hit every time. When she rolled she fell on her side headlong, and she would be righted back by such a demolishing blow that Jukes felt her reeling as a clubbed man reels before he collapses. The gale howled and scuffled about gigantically in the darkness, as though the entire world were one black gully. At certain moments the air streamed against the ship as if sucked through a tunnel with a concentrated solid force of impact that seemed to lift her clean out of the water and keep her up for an instant with only a quiver running through her from end to end. And then she would begin her tumbling again as if dropped back into a boiling cauldron. Jukes tried hard to compose his mind and judge things coolly.

The sea, flattened down in the heavier gusts, would uprise and overwhelm both ends of the Nan-Shan in snowy rushes of foam, expanding wide, beyond both rails, into the night. And on this dazzling sheet, spread under the blackness of the clouds and emitting a bluish glow, Captain MacWhirr could catch a desolate glimpse of a few tiny specks black as ebony, the tops of the hatches, the battened companions, the heads of the covered winches, the foot of a mast. This was all he could see of his ship. Her middle structure, covered by the bridge which bore him, his mate, the closed wheelhouse where a man was steering shut up with the fear of being swept overboard together with the whole thing in one great crash—her middle structure was like a half-tide rock awash upon a coast. It was like an outlying rock with the water boiling up, streaming over, pouring off, beating round—like a rock in the surf to which shipwrecked people cling before they let go—only it rose, it sank, it rolled continuously, without respite and rest, like a rock that should have miraculously struck adrift from a coast and gone wallowing upon the sea.

The Nan-Shan was being looted by the storm with a senseless, destructive fury: trysails torn out of the extra gaskets, double-lashed awnings blown away, bridge swept clean, weather-cloths burst, rails twisted, light-screens smashed—and two of the boats had gone already. They had gone unheard and unseen, melting, as it were, in the shock and smother of the wave. It was only later, when upon the white flash of another high sea hurling itself amidships, Jukes had a vision of two pairs of davits leaping black and empty out of the solid blackness, with one overhauled fall flying and an iron-bound block capering in the air, that he became aware of what had happened within about three yards of his back.

He poked his head forward, groping for the ear of his commander. His lips touched it—big, fleshy, very wet. He cried in an agitated tone, 'Our boats are going now, sir.'

And again he heard that voice, forced and ringing feebly, but with a penetrating effect of quietness in the enormous discord of noises, as if sent out from some remote spot of peace beyond the black wastes of the gale; again he heard a man's voice—the frail and indomitable sound that can be made to carry an infinity of thought, resolution and purpose, that shall be pronouncing confident words on the last day, when heavens fall, and justice is done—again he heard it, and it was crying to him, as if from very, very far—'All right.'

He thought he had not managed to make himself understood. 'Our boats—I say boats—the boats, sir! Two gone!'

The same voice, within a foot of him and yet so remote, yelled sensibly, 'Can't be helped.'

Captain MacWhirr had never turned his face, but Jukes caught some more words on the wind.

'What can—expect—when hammering through—such—Bound to leave—something behind—stands to reason.'

Watchfully Jukes listened for more. No more came. This was all Captain MacWhirr had to say; and Jukes could picture to himself rather than see the broad squat back before him. An impenetrable obscurity pressed down upon the ghostly glimmers of the sea. A dull conviction seized upon Jukes that there was nothing to be done.

If the steering-gear did not give way, if the immense volumes of water did not burst the deck in or smash one of the hatches, if the engines did not give up, if way could be kept on the ship against this terrific wind, and she did not bury herself in one of these awful seas, of whose white crests alone, topping high above her bows, he could now and then get a sickening glimpse—then there was a chance of her coming out of it. Something within him seemed to turn over, bringing uppermost the feeling that the Nan-Shan was lost.

'She's done for,' he said to himself, with a surprising mental agitation, as though he had discovered an unexpected meaning in this thought. One of these things was bound to happen. Nothing could be prevented now, and nothing could be remedied. The men on board did not count, and the ship could not last. This weather was too impossible.

Jukes felt an arm thrown heavily over his shoulders; and to this overture he responded with great intelligence by catching hold of his captain round the waist.

They stood clasped thus in the blind night, bracing each other against the wind, cheek to cheek and lip to ear, in the manner of two hulks lashed stem to stern together.

And Jukes heard the voice of his commander hardly any louder than before, but nearer, as though, starting to march athwart the prodigious rush of the hurricane, it had approached him, bearing that strange effect of quietness like the serene glow of a halo.

'D'ye know where the hands got to?' it asked, vigorous and evanescent at the same time, overcoming the strength of the wind, and swept away from Jukes instantly.

Jukes didn't know. They were all on the bridge when the real force of the hurricane struck the ship. He had no idea where they had crawled to. Under the circumstances they were nowhere, for all the use that could be made of them. Somehow the Captain's wish to know distressed Jukes.

'Want the hands, sir?' he cried, apprehensively.

'Ought to know,' asserted Captain MacWhirr. 'Hold hard.'

They held hard. An outburst of unchained fury, a vicious rush of the wind absolutely steadied the ship; she rocked only, quick and light like a child's cradle, for a terrific moment of suspense, while the whole atmosphere, as it seemed, streamed furiously past her, roaring away from the tenebrous earth.

It suffocated them, and with eyes shut they tightened their grasp. What from the magnitude of the shock might have been a column of water running upright in the dark, butted against the ship, broke short, and fell on her bridge, crushingly, from on high, with a dead burying weight.

A flying fragment of that collapse, a mere splash, enveloped them in one swirl from their feet over their heads, filling violently their ears, mouths and nostrils with salt water. It knocked out their legs, wrenched in haste at their arms, seethed away swiftly under their chins; and opening their eyes, they saw the piled-up masses of foam dashing to and fro amongst what looked like the fragments of a ship. She had given way as if driven straight in. Their panting hearts yielded, too, before the tremendous blow; and all at once she sprang up again to her desperate plunging, as if trying to scramble out from under the ruins.

The seas in the dark seemed to rush from all sides to keep

her back where she might perish. There was hate in the way she was handled, and a ferocity in the blows that fell. She was like a living creature thrown to the rage of a mob: hustled terribly, struck at, borne up, flung down, leaped upon. Captain MacWhirr and Jukes kept hold of each other, deafened by the noise, gagged by the wind; and the great physical tumult beating about their bodies, brought, like an unbridled display of passion, a profound trouble to their souls. One of those wild and appalling shrieks that are heard at times passing mysteriously overhead in the steady roar of a hurricane, swooped, as if borne on wings, upon the ship, and Jukes tried to outscream it.

'Will she live through this?'

The cry was wrenched out of his breast. It was as unintentional as the birth of a thought in the head, and he heard nothing of it himself. It all became extinct at once—thought, intention, effort—and of his cry the inaudible vibration added to the tempest waves of the air.

He expected nothing from it. Nothing at all. For indeed what answer could be made? But after a while he heard with amazement the frail and resisting voice in his ear, the dwarf sound, unconquered in the giant tumult.

'She may!'

It was a dull yell, more difficult to seize than a whisper. And presently the voice returned again, half submerged in the vast crashes, like a ship battling against the waves of an ocean.

'Let's hope so!' it cried—small, lonely and unmoved, a stranger to the visions of hope or fear; and it flickered into disconnected words: 'Ship...This...Never—Anyhow...for the best.' Jukes gave it up.

Then, as if it had come suddenly upon the one thing fit to withstand the power of a storm, it seemed to gain force and firmness for the last broken shouts:

'Keep on hammering...builders...good men...And chance it...engines...Rout...good man.'

Captain MacWhirr removed his arm from Jukes' shoulders, and thereby ceased to exist for his mate, so dark it was; Jukes, after a tense stiffening of every muscle, would let himself go limp all over. The gnawing of profound discomfort existed side by side with an incredible disposition to somnolence, as though he had been buffeted and worried into drowsiness. The wind would get hold of his head and try to shake it off his shoulders; his clothes, full of water, were as heavy as lead, cold and dripping like an armour of melting ice: he shivered—it lasted a long time; and with his hands closed hard on his hold, he was letting himself sink slowly into the depths of bodily misery. His mind became concentrated upon himself in an aimless, idle way, and when something pushed lightly at the back of his knees he nearly, as the saying is, jumped out of his skin.

In the start forward he bumped the back of Captain MacWhirr, who didn't move; and then a hand gripped his thigh. A lull had come, a menacing lull of the wind, the holding of a stormy breath—and he felt himself pawed all over. It was the boatswain. Jukes recognized these hands, so thick and enormous that they seemed to belong to some new species of man.

The boatswain had arrived on the bridge, crawling on all fours against the wind, and had found the chief mate's legs with the top of his head. Immediately he crouched and began to explore Jukes' person upwards with prudent, apologetic touches, as became an inferior.

He was an ill-favoured, undersized, gruff sailor of fifty, coarsely hairy, short-legged, long-armed, resembling an elderly ape. His strength was immense; and in his great lumpy paws, bulging like brown boxing-gloves on the end of furry forearms, the heaviest objects were handled like playthings. Apart from the grizzled pelt on his chest, the menacing demeanour and the hoarse voice, he had none of the classical attributes of his rating. His good nature almost amounted to imbecility: the men did what they liked with him, and he had not an ounce of initiative in his character, which was easy-going and talkative. For these reasons Jukes disliked him; but Captain MacWhirr, to Jukes' scornful disgust, seemed to regard him as a first-rate petty officer.

He pulled himself up by Jukes' coat, taking that liberty with the greatest moderation, and only so far as it was forced upon him by the hurricane.

'What is it, boss'n, what is it?' yelled Jukes, impatiently. What could that fraud of a boss'n want on the bridge? The typhoon had got on Jukes' nerves. The husky bellowings of the other, though unintelligible, seemed to suggest a state of lively satisfaction.

There could be no mistake. The old fool was pleased with something.

The boatswain's other hand had found some other body, for in a changed tone he began to inquire: 'Is it you, sir? Is it you, sir?' The wind strangled his howls.

'Yes!' cried Captain MacWhirr.

IV

All that the boatswain, out of a superabundance of yells, could make clear to Captain MacWhirr was the bizarre intelligence that 'All them Chinamen in the fore 'tween deck have fetched away, sir.'

Jukes to leeward could hear these two shouting within six inches of his face, as you may hear on a still night half a mile away two men conversing across a field. He heard Captain MacWhirr's exasperated 'What? What?' and the strained pitch of the other's hoarseness. 'In a lump…seen them myself…Awful sight, sir…thought…tell you.'

Jukes remained indifferent, as if rendered irresponsible by the force of the hurricane, which made the very thought of action utterly vain. Besides, being very young, he had found the occupation of keeping his heart completely steeled against the worst so engrossing that he had come to feel an overpowering dislike towards any other form of activity whatever. He was not scared; he knew this because, firmly believing he would never see another sunrise, he remained calm in that belief.

These are the moments of do-nothing heroics to which even good men surrender at times. Many officers of ships can no doubt recall a case in their experience when just such a trance of confounded stoicism would come all at once over a whole ship's company. Jukes, however, had no wide experience of men or storms. He conceived himself to be calm—inexorably calm; but as a matter of fact he was daunted; not abjectly, but only so far as a decent man may, without becoming loathsome to himself.

It was rather like a forced-on numbness of spirit. The long, long stress of a gale does it; the suspense of the interminably culminating catastrophe; and there is a bodily fatigue in the mere holding on to existence within the excessive tumult; a searching and insidious fatigue that penetrates deep into a man's breast to cast down and sadden his heart, which is incorrigible, and of all the gifts of the earth—even before life itself—aspires to peace.

Jukes was benumbed much more than he supposed. He held on—very wet, very cold, stiff in every limb; and in a momentary hallucination of swift visions (it is said that a drowning man thus reviews all his life) he beheld all sorts of memories altogether unconnected with his present situation. He remembered his father, for instance: a worthy business man, who at an unfortunate crisis in his affairs went quietly to bed and died forthwith in a state of resignation. Jukes did not recall these circumstances, of course, but remaining otherwise unconcerned he seemed to see distinctly the poor man's face; a certain game of nap played when quite a boy in Table Bay on board a ship, since lost with all hands; the thick eyebrows of his first skipper; and without any emotion, as he might years ago have walked listlessly into her room and found her sitting there with a book, he remembered his mother—dead, too, now—the resolute woman, left badly off, who had been very firm in his bringing up.

It could not have lasted more than a second, perhaps not so much. A heavy arm had fallen about his shoulders; Captain MacWhirr's voice was speaking his name into his ear.

'Jukes! Jukes!'

He detected the tone of deep concern. The wind had thrown its weight on the ship, trying to pin her down amongst the seas. They made a clean breach over her, as over a deep-swimming log; and the gathered weight of crashes menaced monstrously from afar. The breakers flung out of the night with a ghostly light on their crests—the light of sea-foam that in a ferocious, boiling-up pale flash showed upon the slender body of the ship the toppling rush, the downfall, and the seething mad scurry of each wave. Never for a moment could she shake herself clear of the water; Jukes, rigid, perceived in her motion the ominous sign of haphazard floundering. She was no longer struggling intelligently. It was the beginning of the end; and the note of busy concern in Captain MacWhirr's voice sickened him like an exhibition of blind and pernicious folly.

The spell of the storm had fallen upon Jukes. He was penetrated by it, absorbed by it; he was rooted in it with a rigour of dumb attention. Captain MacWhirr persisted in his cries, but the wind got between them like a solid wedge. He hung round Jukes' neck as heavy as a millstone, and suddenly the sides of their heads knocked together.

'Jukes! Mr Jukes, I say!'

He had to answer that voice that would not be silenced. He answered in the customary manner: '...Yes, sir.'

And directly, his heart, corrupted by the storm that breeds a craving for peace, rebelled against the tyranny of training and command.

Captain MacWhirr had his mate's head fixed firm in the crook of his elbow, and pressed it to his yelling lips mysteriously. Sometimes Jukes would break in, admonishing hastily: 'Look out, sir!' or Captain MacWhirr would bawl an earnest exhortation to 'Hold hard, there!' and the whole black universe seemed to reel together with the ship. They paused. She floated yet. And Captain MacWhirr would resume, his shouts. '...Says...whole lot...fetched away...Ought to see...what's the matter.'

Directly the full force of the hurricane had struck the ship, every part of her deck became untenable; and the sailors, dazed and dismayed, took shelter in the port alleyway under the bridge. It had a door aft, which they shut; it was very black, cold and dismal. At each heavy fling of the ship they would groan all together in the dark, and tons of water could be heard scuttling about as if trying to get at them from above. The boatswain had been keeping up a gruff talk, but a more unreasonable lot of men, he said afterwards, he had never been with. They were snug enough there, out of harm's way, and not wanted to do anything, either; and yet they did nothing but grumble and complain peevishly like so many sick kids. Finally, one of them said that if there had been at least some light to see each other's noses by, it wouldn't be so bad. It was making him crazy, he declared, to lie there in the dark waiting for the blamed hooker to sink.

'Why don't you step outside, then, and be done with it at once?' the boatswain turned on him.

This called up a shout of execration. The boatswain found himself overwhelmed with reproaches of all sorts. They seemed to take it ill that a lamp was not instantly created for them out of nothing. They would whine after a light to get drowned by—anyhow! And though the unreason of their revilings was patent—since no one could hope to reach the lamp-room, which was forward—he became greatly distressed. He did not think it was decent of them to be nagging at him like this. He told them so, and was met by general contumely. He sought refuge, therefore, in an embittered silence. At the same time their grumbling and sighing and muttering worried him greatly, but by-and-by it occurred to him that there were six globe lamps hung in the 'tween-deck, and that there could be no harm in depriving the coolies of one of them.

The Nan-Shan had an athwartship coal-bunker, which, being at times used as cargo space, communicated by an iron door with the fore 'tween-deck. It was empty then, and its manhole was the foremost one in the alleyway. The boatswain could get in, therefore, without coming out on deck at all; but to his great surprise he found he could induce no one to help him in taking off the manhole cover. He groped for it all the same, but one of the crew lying in his way refused to budge.

'Why, I only want to get you that blamed light you are

crying for,' he expostulated, almost pitifully.

Somebody told him to go and put his head in a bag. He regretted he could not recognize the voice, and that it was too dark to see, otherwise, as he said, he would have put a head on that son of a sea-cook, anyway, sink or swim. Nevertheless, he had made up his mind to show them he could get a light, if he were to die for it.

Through the violence of the ship's rolling, every movement was dangerous. To be lying down seemed labour enough. He nearly broke his neck dropping into the bunker. He fell on his back, and was sent shooting helplessly from side to side in the dangerous company of a heavy iron bar—a coal-trimmer's slice probably—left down there by somebody. This thing made him as nervous as though it had been a wild beast. He could not see it, the inside of the bunker coated with coal-dust being perfectly and impenetrably black; but he heard it sliding and clattering, and striking here and there, always in the neighbourhood of his head. It seemed to make an extraordinary noise, too—to give heavy thumps as though it had been as big as a bridge girder. This was remarkable enough for him to notice while he was flung from port to starboard and back again, and clawing desperately the smooth sides of the bunker in the endeavour to stop himself. The door into the 'tween-deck not fitting quite true, he saw a thread of dim light at the bottom.

Being a sailor, and a still active man, he did not want much of a chance to regain his feet; and as luck would have it, in scrambling up he put his hand on the iron slice, picking it up as he rose. Otherwise he would have been afraid of the thing breaking his legs, or at least knocking him down again. At first he stood still. He felt unsafe in this darkness that seemed to make the ship's motion unfamiliar, unforeseen, and difficult to counteract. He felt so much shaken for a moment that he dared not move for fear of 'taking charge again.' He had no mind to get battered to pieces in that bunker.

He had struck his head twice; he was dazed a little. He seemed to hear yet so plainly the clatter and bangs of the iron slice flying about his ears that he tightened his grip to prove to himself he had it there safely in his hand. He was vaguely amazed at the plainness with which down there he could hear the gale raging. Its howls and shrieks seemed to take on, in the emptiness of the bunker, something of the human character, of human rage and pain—being not vast but infinitely poignant. And there were, with every roll, thumps, too—profound, ponderous thumps, as if a bulky object of five-ton weight or so had got play in the hold. But there was no such thing in the cargo. Something on deck? Impossible. Or alongside? Couldn't be.

He thought all this quickly, clearly, competently, like a seaman, and in the end remained puzzled. This noise, though, came deadened from outside, together with the washing and pouring of water on deck above his head. Was it the wind? Must be. It made down there a row like the shouting of a big lot of crazed men. And he discovered in himself a desire for a light, too—if only to get drowned by—and a nervous anxiety to get out of that bunker as quickly as possible.

He pulled back the bolt: the heavy iron plate turned on its hinges; and it was as though he had opened the door to the sounds of the tempest. A gust of hoarse yelling met him: the air was still; and the rushing of water overhead was covered by a tumult of strangled, throaty shrieks that produced an effect of desperate confusion. He straddled his legs the whole width of the doorway and stretched his neck. And at first he perceived only what he had come to seek: six small yellow flames swinging violently on the great body of the dusk.

It was stayed like the gallery of a mine, with a row of stanchions in the middle, and cross-beams overhead, penetrating into the gloom ahead—indefinitely. And to port there loomed, like the caving in of one of the sides, a bulky mass with a slanting outline. The whole place, with the shadows and the shapes, moved all the time. The boatswain glared: the ship lurched to starboard, and a great howl came from that mass that had the slant of fallen earth.

Pieces of wood whizzed past. Planks, he thought, inexpressibly startled, and flinging back his head. At his feet a man went sliding over, open-eyed, on his back, straining with uplifted arms for nothing: and another came bounding like a detached stone with his head between his legs and his hands clenched. His pigtail whipped in the air; he made a grab at the boatswain's legs, and from his opened hand a bright white disc rolled against the boatswain's foot. He recognized a silver dollar, and yelled at it with astonishment. With a precipitated sound of trampling and shuffling of bare feet, and with guttural cries, the mound of writhing bodies piled up to port detached itself from the ship's side and sliding, inert and struggling, shifted to starboard, with a dull, brutal thump. The cries ceased. The boatswain heard a long moan through the roar and whistling of the wind; he saw an inextricable confusion of heads and shoulders, naked soles kicking upwards, fists raised, tumbling backs, legs, pigtails, faces.

'Good Lord!' he cried, horrified, and banged-to the iron door upon this vision.

This was what he had come on the bridge to tell. He could not keep it to himself; and on board ship there is only one man to whom it is worth while to unburden yourself. On his passage back the hands in the alleyway swore at him for a fool.

Why didn't he bring that lamp? What the devil did the coolies matter to anybody? And when he came out, the extremity of the ship made what went on inside of her appear of little moment.

At first he thought he had left the alleyway in the very moment of her sinking. The bridge ladders had been washed away, but an enormous sea filling the after-deck floated him up. After that he had to lie on his stomach for some time, holding to a ring-bolt, getting his breath now and then, and swallowing salt water. He struggled farther on his hands and knees, too frightened and distracted to turn back. In this way he reached the after-part of the wheelhouse. In that comparatively sheltered spot he found the second mate.

The boatswain was pleasantly surprised—his impression being that everybody on deck must have been washed away a long time ago. He asked eagerly where the Captain was.

The second mate was lying low, like a malignant little animal under a hedge.

'Captain? Gone overboard, after getting us into this mess.' The mate, too, for all he knew or cared. Another fool. Didn't matter. Everybody was going by-and-by.

The boatswain crawled out again into the strength of the wind; not because he much expected to find anybody, he said, but just to get away from 'that man.' He crawled out as outcasts go to face an inclement world. Hence his great joy at finding Jukes and the Captain. But what was going on in the 'tween-deck was to him a minor matter by that time. Besides, it was difficult to make yourself heard. But he managed to convey the idea that the Chinaman had broken adrift together with their boxes, and that he had come up on purpose to report this. As to the hands, they were all right. Then, appeased, he subsided on the deck in a sitting posture, hugging with his arms and legs the stand of the engine-room telegraph—an iron casting as thick as a post. When that went, why, he expected he would go, too. He gave no more thought to the coolies.

Captain MacWhirr had made Jukes understand that he wanted him to go down below—to see.

'What am I to do then, sir?' And the trembling of his whole wet body caused Jukes' voice to sound like bleating.

'See first…Boss'n…says…adrift.'

'That boss'n is a confounded fool,' howled Jukes, shakily.

The absurdity of the demand made upon him revolted Jukes. He was as unwilling to go as if the moment he had left the deck the ship were sure to sink.

'I must know…can't leave…'

'They'll settle, sir.'

'Fight…boss'n says they fight…Why? Can't have…fighting…board ship…Much rather keep you here…case…I should…washed overboard myself…Stop it…some way. You see and tell me…through engine-room tube. Don't want you…come up here…too often. Dangerous…moving about…deck.'

Jukes, held with his head in chancery, had to listen to what seemed horrible suggestions.

'Don't want…you get lost…so long…ship isn't…Rout…Good man…Ship…may…through this…all right yet.'

All at once Jukes understood he would have to go.

'Do you think she may?' he screamed.

But the wind devoured the reply, out of which Jukes heard only the one word, pronounced with great energy '…Always…'

Captain MacWhirr released Jukes, and bending over the boatswain, yelled, 'Get back with the mate.' Jukes only knew that the arm was gone off his shoulders. He was dismissed with his orders—to do what? He was exasperated into letting go his hold carelessly, and on the instant was blown away. It seemed to him that nothing could stop him from being blown right over the stern. He flung himself down hastily, and the boatswain, who was following, fell on him.

'Don't you get up yet, sir,' cried the boatswain. 'No hurry!'

A sea swept over. Jukes understood the boatswain to splutter that the bridge ladders were gone. 'I'll lower you down, sir, by your hands,' he screamed. He shouted also something about the smoke-stack being as likely to go overboard as not. Jukes thought it very possible, and imagined the fires out, the ship helpless...The boatswain by his side kept on yelling. 'What? What is it?' Jukes cried distressfully; and the other repeated, 'What would my old woman say if she saw me now?'

In the alleyway, where a lot of water had got in and splashed in the dark, the men were still as death, till Jukes stumbled against one of them and cursed him savagely for being in the way. Two or three voices then asked, eager and weak, 'Any chance for us, sir?'

'What's the matter with you fools?' he said brutally. He felt as though he could throw himself down amongst them and never move any more. But they seemed cheered; and in the midst of obsequious warnings, 'Look out! Mind that manhole lid, sir,' they lowered him into the bunker. The boatswain tumbled down after him, and as soon as he had picked himself up he remarked, 'She would say, 'Serve you right, you old fool, for going to sea."

The boatswain had some means, and made a point of alluding to them frequently. His wife—a fat woman—and two grown-up daughters kept a greengrocer's shop in the East-end of London.

In the dark, Jukes, unsteady on his legs, listened to a faint thunderous patter. A deadened screaming went on steadily at his elbow, as it were; and from above the louder tumult of the storm descended upon these near sounds. His head swam. To him, too, in that bunker, the motion of the ship seemed novel and menacing, sapping his resolution as though he had never been afloat before.

He had half a mind to scramble out again; but the remembrance of Captain MacWhirr's voice made this impossible. His orders were to go and see. What was the good of it, he wanted to know. Enraged, he told himself he would see—of course. But the boatswain, staggering clumsily, warned him to be careful how he opened that door; there was a blamed fight going on. And Jukes, as if in great bodily pain, desired irritably to know what the devil they were fighting for.

'Dollars! Dollars, sir. All their rotten chests got burst open. Blamed money skipping all over the place, and they are tumbling after it head over heels—tearing and biting like anything. A regular little hell in there.'

Jukes convulsively opened the door. The short boatswain peered under his arm.

One of the lamps had gone out, broken perhaps. Rancorous, guttural cries burst out loudly on their ears, and a strange panting sound, the working of all these straining breasts. A hard blow hit the side of the ship: water fell above with a stunning shock, and in the forefront of the gloom, where the air was reddish and thick, Jukes saw a head bang the deck violently, two thick calves waving on high, muscular arms twined round a naked body, a yellow-face, open-mouthed and with a set wild stare, look up and slide away. An empty chest clattered turning over; a man fell head first with a jump, as if lifted by a kick; and farther off, indistinct, others streamed like a mass of rolling stones down a bank, thumping the deck with their feet and flourishing their arms wildly. The hatchway ladder was loaded with coolies swarming on it like bees on a branch. They hung on the steps in a crawling, stirring cluster, beating madly with their fists the underside of the battened hatch, and the headlong rush of the water above was heard in the intervals of their yelling. The ship heeled over more, and they began to drop off: first one, then two, then all the rest went away together, falling straight off with a great cry.

Jukes was confounded. The boatswain, with gruff anxiety, begged him, 'Don't you go in there, sir.'

The whole place seemed to twist upon itself, jumping incessantly the while; and when the ship rose to a sea Jukes fancied that all these men would be shot upon him in a body. He backed out, swung the door to, and with trembling hands pushed at the bolt...

As soon as his mate had gone Captain MacWhirr, left alone on the bridge, sidled and staggered as far as the wheelhouse. Its door being hinged forward, he had to fight the gale for admittance, and when at last he managed to enter, it was with an instantaneous clatter and a bang, as though he had been fired through the wood. He stood within, holding on to the handle.

The steering-gear leaked steam, and in the confined space the glass of the binnacle made a shiny oval of light in a thin white fog. The wind howled, hummed, whistled, with sudden booming gusts that rattled the doors and shutters in the vicious patter of sprays. Two coils of lead-line and a small canvas bag hung on a long lanyard, swung wide off, and came back clinging to the bulkheads. The gratings underfoot were nearly afloat; with every sweeping blow of a sea, water squirted violently through the cracks all round the door, and the man at the helm had flung down his cap, his coat, and stood propped against the gear-casing in a striped cotton shirt open on his breast. The little brass wheel in his hands had the appearance of a bright and fragile toy. The cords of his neck stood hard and lean, a dark patch lay in the hollow of his throat, and his face was still and sunken as in death.

Captain MacWhirr wiped his eyes. The sea that had nearly taken him overboard had, to his great annoyance, washed his sou'-wester hat off his bald head. The fluffy, fair hair, soaked and darkened, resembled a mean skein of cotton threads festooned round his bare skull. His face, glistening with sea-water, had been made crimson with the wind, with the sting of sprays. He looked as though he had come off sweating from before a furnace.

'You here?' he muttered, heavily.

The second mate had found his way into the wheelhouse some time before. He had fixed himself in a corner with his knees up, a fist pressed against each temple; and this attitude suggested rage, sorrow, resignation, surrender, with a sort of concentrated unforgiveness. He said mournfully and defiantly, 'Well, it's my watch below now: ain't it?'

The steam gear clattered, stopped, clattered again; and the helmsman's eyeballs seemed to project out of a hungry face as if the compass card behind the binnacle glass had been meat. God knows how long he had been left there to steer, as if forgotten by all his shipmates. The bells had not been struck; there had been no reliefs; the ship's routine had gone down wind; but he was trying to keep her head north-north-east. The rudder might have been gone for all he knew, the fires out, the engines broken down, the ship ready to roll over like a corpse. He was anxious not to get muddled and lose control of her head, because the compass-card swung far both ways, wriggling on the pivot, and sometimes seemed to whirl right round. He suffered from mental stress. He was horribly afraid, also, of the wheelhouse going. Mountains of water kept on tumbling against it. When the ship took one of her desperate dives the corners of his lips twitched.

Captain MacWhirr looked up at the wheelhouse clock. Screwed to the bulk-head, it had a white face on which the black hands appeared to stand quite still. It was half-past one in the morning.

'Another day,' he muttered to himself.

The second mate heard him, and lifting his head as one grieving amongst ruins, 'You won't see it break,' he exclaimed. His wrists and his knees could be seen to shake violently. 'No, by God! You won't…'

He took his face again between his fists.

The body of the helmsman had moved slightly, but his head didn't budge on his neck,—like a stone head fixed to look one way from a column. During a roll that all but took his booted legs from under him, and in the very stagger to save himself, Captain MacWhirr said austerely, 'Don't you pay any attention to what that man says.' And then, with an indefinable change of tone, very grave, he added, 'He isn't on duty.'

The sailor said nothing.

The hurricane boomed, shaking the little place, which seemed air-tight; and the light of the binnacle flickered all the time.

'You haven't been relieved,' Captain MacWhirr went on, looking down. 'I want you to stick to the helm, though, as long as you can. You've got the hang of her. Another man coming here might make a mess of it. Wouldn't do. No child's play.

And the hands are probably busy with a job down below... Think you can?'

The steering-gear leaped into an abrupt short clatter, stopped smouldering like an ember; and the still man, with a motionless gaze, burst out, as if all the passion in him had gone into his lips: 'By Heavens, sir! I can steer for ever if nobody talks to me.'

'Oh! aye! All right...' The Captain lifted his eyes for the first time to the man, '...Hackett.'

And he seemed to dismiss this matter from his mind. He stooped to the engine-room speaking-tube, blew in, and bent his head. Mr Rout below answered, and at once Captain MacWhirr put his lips to the mouthpiece.

With the uproar of the gale around him he applied alternately his lips and his ear, and the engineer's voice mounted to him, harsh and as if out of the heat of an engagement. One of the stokers was disabled, the others had given in, the second engineer and the donkey-man were firing-up. The third engineer was standing by the steam-valve. The engines were being tended by hand. How was it above?

'Bad enough. It mostly rests with you,' said Captain MacWhirr. Was the mate down there yet? No? Well, he would be presently. Would Mr Rout let him talk through the speaking-tube?—through the deck speaking-tube, because he—the Captain—was going out again on the bridge directly. There was some trouble amongst the Chinamen. They were fighting, it seemed. Couldn't allow fighting anyhow...

Mr Rout had gone away, and Captain MacWhirr could feel against his ear the pulsation of the engines, like the beat of the ship's heart. Mr Rout's voice down there shouted something distantly. The ship pitched headlong, the pulsation leaped with a hissing tumult, and stopped dead. Captain MacWhirr's face was impassive, and his eyes were fixed aimlessly on the crouching shape of the second mate. Again Mr Rout's voice cried out in the depths, and the pulsating beats recommenced, with slow strokes—growing swifter.

Mr Rout had returned to the tube. 'It don't matter much what they do,' he said, hastily; and then, with irritation, 'She takes these dives as if she never meant to come up again.'

'Awful sea,' said the Captain's voice from above.

'Don't let me drive her under,' barked Solomon Rout up the pipe.

'Dark and rain. Can't see what's coming,' uttered the voice. 'Must—keep—her—moving—enough to steer—and chance it,' it went on to state distinctly.

'I am doing as much as I dare.'

'We are—getting—smashed up—a good deal up here,' proceeded the voice mildly. 'Doing—fairly well—though. Of course, if the wheelhouse should go...'

Mr Rout, bending an attentive ear, muttered peevishly something under his breath.

But the deliberate voice up there became animated to ask: 'Jukes turned up yet?' Then, after a short wait, 'I wish he would bear a hand. I want him to be done and come up here in case of anything. To look after the ship. I am all alone. The second mate's lost...'

'What?' shouted Mr Rout into the engine-room, taking his head away. Then up the tube he cried, 'Gone overboard?' and clapped his ear to.

'Lost his nerve,' the voice from above continued in a matter-of-fact tone. 'Damned awkward circumstance.'

Mr Rout, listening with bowed neck, opened his eyes wide at this. However, he heard something like the sounds of a scuffle and broken exclamations coming down to him. He strained his hearing; and all the time Beale, the third engineer, with his arms uplifted, held between the palms of his hands the rim of a little black wheel projecting at the side of a big copper pipe.

He seemed to be poising it above his head, as though it were a correct attitude in some sort of game.

To steady himself, he pressed his shoulder against the white bulkhead, one knee bent, and a sweat-rag tucked in his belt hanging on his hip. His smooth cheek was begrimed and flushed, and the coal dust on his eyelids, like the black pencilling of a make-up, enhanced the liquid brilliance of the whites, giving to his youthful face something of a feminine, exotic and fascinating aspect. When the ship pitched he would with hasty movements of his hands screw hard at the little wheel.

'Gone crazy,' began the Captain's voice suddenly in the tube. 'Rushed at me…Just now. Had to knock him down… This minute. You heard, Mr Rout?'

'The devil!' muttered Mr Rout. 'Look out, Beale!'

His shout rang out like the blast of a warning trumpet, between the iron walls of the engine-room. Painted white, they rose high into the dusk of the skylight, sloping like a roof; and the whole lofty space resembled the interior of a monument, divided by floors of iron grating, with lights flickering at different levels, and a mass of gloom lingering in the middle, within the columnar stir of machinery under the motionless swelling of the cylinders. A loud and wild resonance, made up of all the noises of the hurricane, dwelt in the still warmth of the air. There was in it the smell of hot metal, of oil, and a slight mist of steam. The blows of the sea seemed to traverse it in an unringing, stunning shock, from side to side.

Gleams, like pale long flames, trembled upon the polish

of metal; from the flooring below the enormous crank-heads emerged in their turns with a flash of brass and steel—going over; while the connecting-rods, big-jointed, like skeleton limbs, seemed to thrust them down and pull them up again with an irresistible precision. And deep in the half-light other rods dodged deliberately to and fro, crossheads nodded, discs of metal rubbed smoothly against each other, slow and gentle, in a commingling of shadows and gleams.

Sometimes all those powerful and unerring movements would slow down simultaneously, as if they had been the functions of a living organism, stricken suddenly by the blight of languor; and Mr Rout's eyes would blaze darker in his long sallow face. He was fighting this fight in a pair of carpet slippers. A short shiny jacket barely covered his loins, and his white wrists protruded far out of the tight sleeves, as though the emergency had added to his stature, had lengthened his limbs, augmented his pallor, hollowed his eyes.

He moved, climbing high up, disappearing low down, with a restless, purposeful industry, and when he stood still, holding the guard-rail in front of the starting-gear, he would keep glancing to the right at the steam-gauge, at the water-gauge, fixed upon the white wall in the light of a swaying lamp. The mouths of two speaking-tubes gaped stupidly at his elbow, and the dial of the engine-room telegraph resembled a clock of large diameter, bearing on its face curt words instead of figures. The grouped letters stood out heavily black, around the pivot-head of the indicator, emphatically symbolic of loud exclamations: AHEAD, ASTERN, SLOW, Half, STAND BY; and the fat black hand pointed downwards to the word FULL, which, thus singled out, captured the eye as a sharp cry secures attention.

The wood-encased bulk of the low-pressure cylinder,

frowning portly from above, emitted a faint wheeze at every thrust, and except for that low hiss the engines worked their steel limbs headlong or slow with a silent, determined smoothness. And all this, the white walls, the moving steel, the floor plates under Solomon Rout's feet, the floors of iron grating above his head, the dusk and the gleams, uprose and sank continuously, with one accord, upon the harsh wash of the waves against the ship's side. The whole loftiness of the place, booming hollow to the great voice of the wind, swayed at the top like a tree, would go over bodily, as if borne down this way and that by the tremendous blasts.

'You've got to hurry up,' shouted Mr Rout, as soon as he saw Jukes appear in the stokehold doorway.

Jukes' glance was wandering and tipsy; his red face was puffy, as though he had overslept himself. He had had an arduous road, and had travelled over it with immense vivacity, the agitation of his mind corresponding to the exertions of his body. He had rushed up out of the bunker, stumbling in the dark alleyway amongst a lot of bewildered men who, trod upon, asked 'What's up, sir?' in awed mutters all round him;—down the stokehold ladder, missing many iron rungs in his hurry, down into a place deep as a well, black as Tophet, tipping over back and forth like a see-saw. The water in the bilges thundered at each roll, and lumps of coal skipped to and fro, from end to end, rattling like an avalanche of pebbles on a slope of iron.

Somebody in there moaned with pain, and somebody else could be seen crouching over what seemed the prone body of a dead man; a lusty voice blasphemed; and the glow under each fire-door was like a pool of flaming blood radiating quietly in a velvety blackness.

A gust of wind struck upon the nape of Jukes' neck and

next moment he felt it streaming about his wet ankles. The stokehold ventilators hummed: in front of the six fire-doors two wild figures, stripped to the waist, staggered and stooped, wrestling with two shovels.

'Hallo! Plenty of draught now,' yelled the second engineer at once, as though he had been all the time looking out for Jukes. The donkeyman, a dapper little chap with a dazzling fair skin and a tiny, gingery moustache, worked in a sort of mute transport. They were keeping a full head of steam, and a profound rumbling, as of an empty furniture van trotting over a bridge, made a sustained bass to all the other noises of the place.

'Blowing off all the time,' went on yelling the second. With a sound as of a hundred scoured saucepans, the orifice of a ventilator spat upon his shoulder a sudden gush of salt water, and he volleyed a stream of curses upon all things on earth including his own soul, ripping and raving, and all the time attending to his business. With a sharp clash of metal the ardent pale glare of the fire opened upon his bullet head, showing his spluttering lips, his insolent face, and with another clang closed like the white-hot wink of an iron eye.

'Where's the blooming ship? Can you tell me? blast my eyes! Under water—or what? It's coming down here in tons. Are the condemned cowls gone to Hades? Hey? Don't you know anything—you jolly sailor-man you...?'

Jukes, after a bewildered moment, had been helped by a roll to dart through; and as soon as his eyes took in the comparative vastness, peace and brilliance of the engine-room, the ship, setting her stern heavily in the water, sent him charging head down upon Mr Rout.

The chief's arm, long like a tentacle, and straightening as if worked by a spring, went out to meet him, and deflected his rush into a spin towards the speaking-tubes. At the same time Mr Rout repeated earnestly:

'You've got to hurry up, whatever it is.'

Jukes yelled 'Are you there, sir?' and listened. Nothing. Suddenly the roar of the wind fell straight into his ear, but presently a small voice shoved aside the shouting hurricane quietly.

'You, Jukes?—Well?'

Jukes was ready to talk: it was only time that seemed to be wanting. It was easy enough to account for everything. He could perfectly imagine the coolies battened down in the reeking 'tween-deck, lying sick and scared between the rows of chests. Then one of these chests—or perhaps several at once—breaking loose in a roll, knocking out others, sides splitting, lids flying open, and all these clumsy Chinamen rising up in a body to save their property. Afterwards every fling of the ship would hurl that tramping, yelling mob here and there, from side to side, in a whirl of smashed wood, torn clothing, rolling dollars. A struggle once started, they would be unable to stop themselves. Nothing could stop them now except main force. It was a disaster. He had seen it, and that was all he could say. Some of them must be dead, he believed. The rest would go on fighting…

He sent up his words, tripping over each other, crowding the narrow tube. They mounted as if into a silence of an enlightened comprehension dwelling alone up there with a storm. And Jukes wanted to be dismissed from the face of that odious trouble intruding on the great need of the ship.

V

He waited. Before his eyes the engines turned with slow labour, that in the moment of going off into a mad fling would stop dead at Mr Rout's shout, 'Look out, Beale!' They paused in an intelligent immobility, stilled in mid-stroke, a heavy crank arrested on the cant, as if conscious of danger and the passage of time. Then, with a 'Now, then!' from the chief, and the sound of a breath expelled through clenched teeth, they would accomplish the interrupted revolution and begin another.

There was the prudent sagacity of wisdom and the deliberation of enormous strength in their movements. This was their work—this patient coaxing of a distracted ship over the fury of the waves and into the very eye of the wind. At times Mr Rout's chin would sink on his breast, and he watched them with knitted eyebrows as if lost in thought.

The voice that kept the hurricane out of Jukes' ear began: 'Take the hands with you...,' and left off unexpectedly.

'What could I do with them, sir?'

A harsh, abrupt, imperious clang exploded suddenly. The three pairs of eyes flew up to the telegraph dial to see the hand jump from FULL to STOP, as if snatched by a devil. And then these three men in the engineroom had the intimate sensation of a check upon the ship, of a strange shrinking, as if she had gathered herself for a desperate leap.

'Stop her!' bellowed Mr Rout.

Nobody—not even Captain MacWhirr, who alone on deck had caught sight of a white line of foam coming on at such a height that he couldn't believe his eyes—nobody was to know the steepness of that sea and the awful depth of the hollow the hurricane had scooped out behind the running wall of water.

It raced to meet the ship, and, with a pause, as of girding the loins, the Nan-Shan lifted her bows and leaped. The flames in all the lamps sank, darkening the engine-room. One went out. With a tearing crash and a swirling, raving tumult, tons of water fell upon the deck, as though the ship had darted under the foot of a cataract.

Down there they looked at each other, stunned.

'Swept from end to end, by God!' bawled Jukes.

She dipped into the hollow straight down, as if going over the edge of the world. The engine-room toppled forward menacingly, like the inside of a tower nodding in an earthquake. An awful racket, of iron things falling, came from the stokehold. She hung on this appalling slant long enough for Beale to drop on his hands and knees and begin to crawl as if he meant to fly on all fours out of the engine-room, and for Mr Rout to turn his head slowly, rigid, cavernous, with the lower jaw dropping. Jukes had shut his eyes, and his face in a moment became hopelessly blank and gentle, like the face of a blind man.

At last she rose slowly, staggering, as if she had to lift a mountain with her bows.

Mr Rout shut his mouth; Jukes blinked; and little Beale stood up hastily.

'Another one like this, and that's the last of her,' cried the chief.

He and Jukes looked at each other, and the same thought came into their heads. The Captain! Everything must have been swept away. Steering-gear gone—ship like a log. All over directly.

'Rush!' ejaculated Mr Rout thickly, glaring with enlarged, doubtful eyes at Jukes, who answered him by an irresolute glance.

The clang of the telegraph gong soothed them instantly. The black hand dropped in a flash from STOP to FULL.

'Now then, Beale!' cried Mr Rout.

The steam hissed low. The piston-rods slid in and out. Jukes put his ear to the tube. The voice was ready for him. It said: 'Pick up all the money. Bear a hand now. I'll want you up here.' And that was all.

'Sir?' called up Jukes. There was no answer.

He staggered away like a defeated man from the field of battle. He had got, in some way or other, a cut above his left eyebrow—a cut to the bone. He was not aware of it in the least: quantities of the China Sea, large enough to break his neck for him, had gone over his head, had cleaned, washed, and salted that wound. It did not bleed, but only gaped red; and this gash over the eye, his dishevelled hair, the disorder of his clothes, gave him the aspect of a man worsted in a fight with fists.

'Got to pick up the dollars.' He appealed to Mr Rout, smiling pitifully at random.

'What's that?' asked Mr Rout, wildly. 'Pick up…? I don't care…' Then, quivering in every muscle, but with an exaggeration of paternal tone, 'Go away now, for God's sake. You deck people'll drive me silly. There's that second mate been going for the old man. Don't you know? You fellows are going wrong for want of something to do…'

At these words Jukes discovered in himself the beginnings of anger. Want of something to do—indeed…Full of hot scorn against the chief, he turned to go the way he had come. In the stokehold the plump donkeyman toiled with his shovel mutely, as if his tongue had been cut out; but the second was carrying on like a noisy, undaunted maniac, who had preserved his skill in the art of stoking under a marine boiler.

'Hallo, you wandering officer! Hey! Can't you get some of your slush-slingers to wind up a few of them ashes? I am getting choked with them here. Curse it! Hallo! Hey! Remember the articles: Sailors and firemen to assist each other. Hey! D'ye hear?'

Jukes was climbing out frantically, and the other, lifting

up his face after him, howled, 'Can't you speak? What are you poking about here for? What's your game, anyhow?'

A frenzy possessed Jukes. By the time he was back amongst the men in the darkness of the alleyway, he felt ready to wring all their necks at the slightest sign of hanging back. The very thought of it exasperated him. He couldn't hang back. They shouldn't.

The impetuosity with which he came amongst them carried them along. They had already been excited and startled at all his comings and goings—by the fierceness and rapidity of his movements; and more felt than seen in his rushes, he appeared formidable—busied with matters of life and death that brooked no delay. At his first word he heard them drop into the bunker one after another obediently, with heavy thumps.

They were not clear as to what would have to be done. 'What is it? What is it?' they were asking each other. The boatswain tried to explain; the sounds of a great scuffle surprised them: and the mighty shocks, reverberating awfully in the black bunker, kept them in mind of their danger. When the boatswain threw open the door it seemed that an eddy of the hurricane, stealing through the iron sides of the ship, had set all these bodies whirling like dust: there came to them a confused uproar, a tempestuous tumult, a fierce mutter, gusts of screams dying away, and the tramping of feet mingling with the blows of the sea.

For a moment they glared amazed, blocking the doorway. Jukes pushed through them brutally. He said nothing, and simply darted in. Another lot of coolies on the ladder, struggling suicidally to break through the battened hatch to a swamped deck, fell off as before, and he disappeared under them like a man overtaken by a landslide.

The boatswain yelled excitedly: 'Come along. Get the mate

out. He'll be trampled to death. Come on.'

They charged in, stamping on breasts, on fingers, on faces, catching their feet in heaps of clothing, kicking broken wood; but before they could get hold of him Jukes emerged waist deep in a multitude of clawing hands. In the instant he had been lost to view, all the buttons of his jacket had gone, its back had got split up to the collar, his waistcoat had been torn open. The central struggling mass of Chinamen went over to the roll, dark, indistinct, helpless, with a wild gleam of many eyes in the dim light of the lamps.

'Leave me alone—damn you. I am all right,' screeched Jukes. 'Drive them forward. Watch your chance when she pitches. Forward with 'em. Drive them against the bulkhead. Jam 'em up.'

The rush of the sailors into the seething 'tween-deck was like a splash of cold water into a boiling cauldron. The commotion sank for a moment.

The bulk of Chinamen were locked in such a compact scrimmage that, linking their arms and aided by an appalling dive of the ship, the seamen sent it forward in one great shove, like a solid block. Behind their backs small clusters and loose bodies tumbled from side to side.

The boatswain performed prodigious feats of strength. With his long arms open, and each great paw clutching at a stanchion, he stopped the rush of seven entwined Chinamen rolling like a boulder. His joints cracked; he said, 'Ha!' and they flew apart. But the carpenter showed the greater intelligence. Without saying a word to anybody he went back into the alleyway, to fetch several coils of cargo gear he had seen there—chain and rope. With these life-lines were rigged.

There was really no resistance. The struggle, however it began, had turned into a scramble of blind panic. If the coolies had started up after their scattered dollars they were by that time fighting only for their footing. They took each other by the throat merely to save themselves from being hurled about. Whoever got a hold anywhere would kick at the others who caught at his legs and hung on, till a roll sent them flying together across the deck.

The coming of the white devils was a terror. Had they come to kill? The individuals torn out of the ruck became very limp in the seamen's hands: some, dragged aside by the heels, were passive, like dead bodies, with open, fixed eyes. Here and there a coolie would fall on his knees as if begging for mercy; several, whom the excess of fear made unruly, were hit with hard fists between the eyes, and cowered; while those who were hurt submitted to rough handling, blinking rapidly without a plaint. Faces streamed with blood; there were raw places on the shaven heads, scratches, bruises, torn wounds, gashes. The broken porcelain out of the chests was mostly responsible for the latter. Here and there a Chinaman, wild-eyed, with his tail unplaited, nursed a bleeding sole.

They had been ranged closely, after having been shaken into submission, cuffed a little to allay excitement, addressed in gruff words of encouragement that sounded like promises of evil. They sat on the deck in ghastly, drooping rows, and at the end the carpenter, with two hands to help him, moved busily from place to place, setting taut and hitching the life-lines. The boatswain, with one leg and one arm embracing a stanchion, struggled with a lamp pressed to his breast, trying to get a light, and growling all the time like an industrious gorilla. The figures of seamen stooped repeatedly, with the movements of gleaners, and everything was being flung into the bunker: clothing, smashed wood, broken china, and the dollars, too, gathered up in men's jackets. Now and then a sailor would stagger towards the doorway with his arms full of rubbish; and dolorous, slanting eyes followed his movements.

With every roll of the ship the long rows of sitting Celestials would sway forward brokenly, and her headlong dives knocked together the line of shaven polls from end to end. When the wash of water rolling on the deck died away for a moment, it seemed to Jukes, yet quivering from his exertions, that in his mad struggle down there he had overcome the wind somehow: that a silence had fallen upon the ship, a silence in which the sea struck thunderously at her sides.

Everything had been cleared out of the 'tween-deck—all the wreckage, as the men said. They stood erect and tottering above the level of heads and drooping shoulders. Here and there a coolie sobbed for his breath. Where the high light fell, Jukes could see the salient ribs of one, the yellow, wistful face of another; bowed necks; or would meet a dull stare directed at his face. He was amazed that there had been no corpses; but the lot of them seemed at their last gasp, and they appeared to him more pitiful than if they had been all dead.

Suddenly one of the coolies began to speak. The light came and went on his lean, straining face; he threw his head up like a baying hound. From the bunker came the sounds of knocking and the tinkle of some dollars rolling loose; he stretched out his arm, his mouth yawned black, and the incomprehensible guttural hooting sounds, that did not seem to belong to a human language, penetrated Jukes with a strange emotion as if a brute had tried to be eloquent.

Two more started mouthing what seemed to Jukes fierce

denunciations; the others stirred with grunts and growls. Jukes ordered the hands out of the 'tweendecks hurriedly. He left last himself, backing through the door, while the grunts rose to a loud murmur and hands were extended after him as after a malefactor. The boatswain shot the bolt, and remarked uneasily, 'Seems as if the wind had dropped, sir.'

The seamen were glad to get back into the alleyway. Secretly each of them thought that at the last moment he could rush out on deck—and that was a comfort. There is something horribly repugnant in the idea of being drowned under a deck. Now they had done with the Chinamen, they again became conscious of the ship's position.

Jukes on coming out of the alleyway found himself up to the neck in the noisy water. He gained the bridge, and discovered he could detect obscure shapes as if his sight had become preternaturally acute. He saw faint outlines. They recalled not the familiar aspect of the Nan-Shan, but something remembered—an old dismantled steamer he had seen years ago rotting on a mudbank. She recalled that wreck.

There was no wind, not a breath, except the faint currents created by the lurches of the ship. The smoke tossed out of the funnel was settling down upon her deck. He breathed it as he passed forward. He felt the deliberate throb of the engines, and heard small sounds that seemed to have survived the great uproar: the knocking of broken fittings, the rapid tumbling of some piece of wreckage on the bridge. He perceived dimly the squat shape of his captain holding on to a twisted bridge-rail, motionless and swaying as if rooted to the planks. The unexpected stillness of the air oppressed Jukes.

'We have done it, sir,' he gasped.

'Thought you would,' said Captain MacWhirr.

'Did you?' murmured Jukes to himself.

'Wind fell all at once,' went on the Captain.

Jukes burst out: 'If you think it was an easy job—'

But his captain, clinging to the rail, paid no attention. 'According to the books the worst is not over yet.'

'If most of them hadn't been half dead with seasickness and fright, not one of us would have come out of that 'tween-deck alive,' said Jukes.

'Had to do what's fair by them,' mumbled MacWhirr, stolidly. 'You don't find everything in books.'

'Why, I believe they would have risen on us if I hadn't ordered the hands out of that pretty quick,' continued Jukes with warmth.

After the whisper of their shouts, their ordinary tones, so distinct, rang out very loud to their ears in the amazing stillness of the air. It seemed to them they were talking in a dark and echoing vault.

Through a jagged aperture in the dome of clouds the light of a few stars fell upon the black sea, rising and falling confusedly. Sometimes the head of a watery cone would topple on board and mingle with the rolling flurry of foam on the swamped deck; and the Nan-Shan wallowed heavily at the bottom of a circular cistern of clouds. This ring of dense vapours, gyrating madly round the calm of the centre, encompassed the ship like a motionless and unbroken wall of an aspect inconceivably sinister. Within, the sea, as if agitated by an internal commotion, leaped in peaked mounds that jostled each other, slapping heavily against her sides; and a low moaning sound, the infinite plaint of the storm's fury, came from beyond the limits of the menacing calm. Captain MacWhirr remained silent, and Jukes' ready ear caught suddenly the faint, long-drawn roar of some immense wave rushing unseen under that thick blackness, which made the appalling boundary of his vision.

'Of course,' he started resentfully, 'they thought we had caught at the chance to plunder them. Of course! You said—pick up the money. Easier said than done. They couldn't tell what was in our heads. We came in, smash—right into the middle of them. Had to do it by a rush.'

'As long as it's done...,' mumbled the Captain, without attempting to look at Jukes. 'Had to do what's fair.'

'We shall find yet there's the devil to pay when this is over,' said Jukes, feeling very sore. 'Let them only recover a bit, and you'll see. They will fly at our throats, sir. Don't forget, sir, she isn't a British ship now. These brutes know it well, too. The damned Siamese flag.'

'We are on board, all the same,' remarked Captain MacWhirr.

'The trouble's not over yet,' insisted Jukes, prophetically, reeling and catching on. 'She's a wreck,' he added, faintly.

'The trouble's not over yet,' assented Captain MacWhirr, half aloud.... 'Look out for her a minute.'

'Are you going off the deck, sir?' asked Jukes, hurriedly, as if the storm were sure to pounce upon him as soon as he had been left alone with the ship.

He watched her, battered and solitary, labouring heavily in a wild scene of mountainous black waters lit by the gleams of distant worlds. She moved slowly, breathing into the still core of the hurricane the excess of her strength in a white cloud of steam—and the deep-toned vibration of the escape was like the defiant trumpeting of a living creature of the sea impatient for the renewal of the contest. It ceased suddenly. The still air moaned. Above Jukes' head a few stars shone into a pit of black vapours. The inky edge of the cloud-disc frowned upon the ship under the patch of glittering sky. The stars, too, seemed to look at her intently, as if for the last time, and the cluster of their splendour sat like a diadem on a lowering brow.

Captain MacWhirr had gone into the chart-room. There was no light there; but he could feel the disorder of that place where he used to live tidily. His armchair was upset. The books had tumbled out on the floor: he scrunched a piece of glass under his boot. He groped for the matches, and found a box on a shelf with a deep ledge. He struck one, and puckering the corners of his eyes, held out the little flame towards the barometer whose glittering top of glass and metals nodded at him continuously.

It stood very low—incredibly low, so low that Captain MacWhirr grunted. The match went out, and hurriedly he extracted another, with thick, stiff fingers.

Again a little flame flared up before the nodding glass and metal of the top. His eyes looked at it, narrowed with attention, as if expecting an imperceptible sign. With his grave face he resembled a booted and misshapen pagan burning incense before the oracle of a Joss. There was no mistake. It was the lowest reading he had ever seen in his life.

Captain MacWhirr emitted a low whistle. He forgot himself till the flame diminished to a blue spark, burnt his fingers and vanished. Perhaps something had gone wrong with the thing!

There was an aneroid glass screwed above the couch. He turned that way, struck another match, and discovered the white face of the other instrument looking at him from the bulkhead, meaningly, not to be gainsaid, as though the wisdom of men were made unerring by the indifference of matter. There was no room for doubt now. Captain MacWhirr pshawed at it, and threw the match down.

The worst was to come, then—and if the books were right this worst would be very bad. The experience of the last six hours had enlarged his conception of what heavy weather could be like. 'It'll be terrific,' he pronounced, mentally. He had not consciously looked at anything by the light of the matches except at the barometer; and yet somehow he had seen that his water-bottle and the two tumblers had been flung out of their stand. It seemed to give him a more intimate knowledge of the tossing the ship had gone through. 'I wouldn't have believed it,' he thought. And his table had been cleared, too; his rulers, his pencils, the inkstand—all the things that had their safe appointed places—they were gone, as if a mischievous hand had plucked them out one by one and flung them on the wet floor. The hurricane had broken in upon the orderly arrangements of his privacy. This had never happened before, and the feeling of dismay reached the very seat of his composure. And the worst was to come yet! He was glad the trouble in the 'tween-deck had been discovered in time. If the ship had to go after all, then, at least, she wouldn't be going to the bottom with a lot of people in her fighting teeth and claw. That would have been odious. And in that feeling there was a humane intention and a vague sense of the fitness of things.

These instantaneous thoughts were yet in their essence heavy and slow, partaking of the nature of the man. He extended his hand to put back the matchbox in its corner of the shelf. There were always matches there—by his order. The steward had his instructions impressed upon him long before. 'A box... just there, see? Not so very full...where I can put my hand on it, steward. Might want a light in a hurry. Can't tell on board ship what you might want in a hurry. Mind, now.'

And of course on his side he would be careful to put it back in its place scrupulously. He did so now, but before he removed his hand it occurred to him that perhaps he would never have occasion to use that box any more. The vividness of the thought checked him and for an infinitesimal fraction of a second his fingers closed again on the small object as though it had been the symbol of all these little habits that chain us to the weary round of life. He released it at last, and letting himself fall on the settee, listened for the first sounds of returning wind.

Not yet. He heard only the wash of water, the heavy splashes, the dull shocks of the confused seas boarding his ship from all sides. She would never have a chance to clear her decks.

But the quietude of the air was startlingly tense and unsafe, like a slender hair holding a sword suspended over his head. By this awful pause the storm penetrated the defences of the man and unsealed his lips. He spoke out in the solitude and the pitch darkness of the cabin, as if addressing another being awakened within his breast.

'I shouldn't like to lose her,' he said half aloud.

He sat unseen, apart from the sea, from his ship, isolated, as if withdrawn from the very current of his own existence, where such freaks as talking to himself surely had no place. His palms reposed on his knees, he bowed his short neck and puffed heavily, surrendering to a strange sensation of weariness he was not enlightened enough to recognize for the fatigue of mental stress.

From where he sat he could reach the door of a washstand locker. There should have been a towel there. There was. Good... He took it out, wiped his face, and afterwards went on rubbing his wet head. He towelled himself with energy in the dark, and then remained motionless with the towel on his knees. A moment passed, of a stillness so profound that no one could have guessed there was a man sitting in that cabin. Then a murmur arose.

'She may come out of it yet.'

When Captain MacWhirr came out on deck, which he did brusquely, as though he had suddenly become conscious of having stayed away too long, the calm had lasted already more than fifteen minutes—long enough to make itself intolerable even to his imagination. Jukes, motionless on the forepart of the bridge, began to speak at once. His voice, blank and forced as though he were talking through hard-set teeth, seemed to flow away on all sides into the darkness, deepening again upon the sea.

'I had the wheel relieved. Hackett began to sing out that he was done. He's lying in there alongside the steering-gear with a face like death. At first I couldn't get anybody to crawl out and relieve the poor devil. That boss'n's worse than no good, I always said. Thought I would have had to go myself and haul out one of them by the neck.'

'Ah, well,' muttered the Captain. He stood watchful by Jukes' side.

'The second mate's in there, too, holding his head. Is he hurt, sir?'

'No—crazy,' said Captain MacWhirr, curtly.

'Looks as if he had a tumble, though.'

'I had to give him a push,' explained the Captain.

Jukes gave an impatient sigh.

'It will come very sudden,' said Captain MacWhirr, 'and from over there, I fancy. God only knows though. These books are only good to muddle your head and make you jumpy. It will be bad, and there's an end. If we only can steam her round in time to meet it...'

A minute passed. Some of the stars winked rapidly and vanished.

'You left them pretty safe?' began the Captain abruptly, as though the silence were unbearable.

'Are you thinking of the coolies, sir? I rigged lifelines all ways across that 'tween-deck.'

'Did you? Good idea, Mr Jukes.'

'I didn't...think you cared to...know,' said Jukes—the lurching of the ship cut his speech as though somebody had been jerking him around while he talked—'how I got on with... that infernal job. We did it. And it may not matter in the end.'

'Had to do what's fair, for all—they are only Chinamen. Give them the same chance with ourselves—hang it all. She isn't lost yet. Bad enough to be shut up below in a gale—'

'That's what I thought when you gave me the job, sir,' interjected Jukes, moodily.

'—without being battered to pieces,' pursued Captain MacWhirr with rising vehemence. 'Couldn't let that go on in my ship, if I knew she hadn't five minutes to live. Couldn't bear it, Mr Jukes.'

A hollow echoing noise, like that of a shout rolling in a rocky chasm, approached the ship and went away again. The last star, blurred, enlarged, as if returning to the fiery mist of its beginning, struggled with the colossal depth of blackness hanging over the ship—and went out.

'Now for it!' muttered Captain MacWhirr. 'Mr Jukes.'

'Here, sir.'

The two men were growing indistinct to each other.

'We must trust her to go through it and come out on the other side. That's plain and straight. There's no room for Captain Wilson's storm-strategy here.'

'No, sir.'

'She will be smothered and swept again for hours,' mumbled the Captain. 'There's not much left by this time above deck for the sea to take away—unless you or me.'

'Both, sir,' whispered Jukes, breathlessly.

'You are always meeting trouble half way, Jukes,' Captain MacWhirr remonstrated quaintly. 'Though it's a fact that the second mate is no good. D'ye hear, Mr Jukes? You would be left alone if…'

Captain MacWhirr interrupted himself, and Jukes, glancing on all sides, remained silent.

'Don't you be put out by anything,' the Captain continued, mumbling rather fast. 'Keep her facing it. They may say what they like, but the heaviest seas run with the wind. Facing it—always facing it—that's the way to get through. You are a young sailor. Face it. That's enough for any man. Keep a cool head.'

'Yes, sir,' said Jukes, with a flutter of the heart.

In the next few seconds the Captain spoke to the engine-room and got an answer.

For some reason Jukes experienced an access of confidence, a sensation that came from outside like a warm breath, and made him feel equal to every demand. The distant muttering of the darkness stole into his ears. He noted it unmoved, out of that sudden belief in himself, as a man safe in a shirt of mail would watch a point.

The ship laboured without intermission amongst the black hills of water, paying with this hard tumbling the price of her life. She rumbled in her depths, shaking a white plummet of steam into the night, and Jukes' thought skimmed like a bird through the engine-room, where Mr Rout—good man—was ready. When the rumbling ceased it seemed to him that there was a pause of every sound, a dead pause in which Captain MacWhirr's voice rang out startlingly.

'What's that? A puff of wind?'—it spoke much louder than Jukes had ever heard it before—'On the bow. That's right. She may come out of it yet.'

The mutter of the winds drew near apace. In the forefront could be distinguished a drowsy waking plaint passing on, and far off the growth of a multiple clamour, marching and expanding. There was the throb as of many drums in it, a vicious rushing note, and like the chant of a tramping multitude.

Jukes could no longer see his captain distinctly. The darkness was absolutely piling itself upon the ship. At most he made out movements, a hint of elbows spread out, of a head thrown up.

Captain MacWhirr was trying to do up the top button of his oilskin coat with unwonted haste. The hurricane, with its power to madden the seas, to sink ships, to uproot trees, to overturn strong walls and dash the very birds of the air to the ground, had found this taciturn man in its path, and, doing its utmost, had managed to wring out a few words. Before the renewed wrath of winds swooped on his ship, Captain MacWhirr was moved to declare, in a tone of vexation, as it were: 'I wouldn't like to lose her.'

He was spared that annoyance.

VI

On A bright sunshiny day, with the breeze chasing her smoke far ahead, the Nan-Shan came into Fu-chau. Her arrival was at once noticed on shore, and the seamen in harbour said: 'Look! Look at that steamer. What's that? Siamese—isn't she? Just look at her!'

She seemed, indeed, to have been used as a running target

for the secondary batteries of a cruiser. A hail of minor shells could not have given her upper works a more broken, torn, and devastated aspect: and she had about her the worn, weary air of ships coming from the far ends of the world—and indeed with truth, for in her short passage she had been very far; sighting, verily, even the coast of the Great Beyond, whence no ship ever returns to give up her crew to the dust of the earth. She was incrusted and gray with salt to the trucks of her masts and to the top of her funnel; as though (as some facetious seaman said) 'the crowd on board had fished her out somewhere from the bottom of the sea and brought her in here for salvage.' And further, excited by the felicity of his own wit, he offered to give five pounds for her—'as she stands.'

Before she had been quite an hour at rest, a meagre little man, with a red-tipped nose and a face cast in an angry mould, landed from a sampan on the quay of the Foreign Concession, and incontinently turned to shake his fist at her.

A tall individual, with legs much too thin for a rotund stomach, and with watery eyes, strolled up and remarked, 'Just left her—eh? Quick work.'

He wore a soiled suit of blue flannel with a pair of dirty cricketing shoes; a dingy gray moustache drooped from his lip, and daylight could be seen in two places between the rim and the crown of his hat.

'Hallo! what are you doing here?' asked the ex-second-mate of the Nan-Shan, shaking hands hurriedly.

'Standing by for a job—chance worth taking—got a quiet hint,' explained the man with the broken hat, in jerky, apathetic wheezes.

The second shook his fist again at the Nan-Shan. 'There's a fellow there that ain't fit to have the command of a scow,' he declared, quivering with passion, while the other looked about listlessly.

'Is there?'

But he caught sight on the quay of a heavy seaman's chest, painted brown under a fringed sailcloth cover, and lashed with new manila line. He eyed it with awakened interest.

'I would talk and raise trouble if it wasn't for that damned Siamese flag. Nobody to go to—or I would make it hot for him. The fraud! Told his chief engineer—that's another fraud for you—I had lost my nerve. The greatest lot of ignorant fools that ever sailed the seas. No! You can't think…'

'Got your money all right?' inquired his seedy acquaintance suddenly.

'Yes. Paid me off on board,' raged the second mate. 'Get your breakfast on shore,' says he.'

'Mean skunk!' commented the tall man, vaguely, and passed his tongue on his lips. 'What about having a drink of some sort?'

'He struck me,' hissed the second mate.

'No! Struck! You don't say?' The man in blue began to bustle about sympathetically. 'Can't possibly talk here. I want to know all about it. Struck—eh? Let's get a fellow to carry your chest. I know a quiet place where they have some bottled beer…'

Mr Jukes, who had been scanning the shore through a pair of glasses, informed the chief engineer afterwards that 'our late second mate hasn't been long in finding a friend. A chap looking uncommonly like a bummer. I saw them walk away together from the quay.'

The hammering and banging of the needful repairs did not disturb Captain MacWhirr. The steward found in the letter he wrote, in a tidy chart-room, passages of such absorbing interest that twice he was nearly caught in the act. But Mrs MacWhirr, in the drawing-room of the forty-pound house, stifled a yawn—perhaps out of self-respect—for she was alone.

She reclined in a plush-bottomed and gilt hammock-chair near a tiled fireplace, with Japanese fans on the mantel and a glow of coals in the grate. Lifting her hands, she glanced wearily here and there into the many pages. It was not her fault they were so prosy, so completely uninteresting—from 'My darling wife' at the beginning, to 'Your loving husband' at the end. She couldn't be really expected to understand all these ship affairs. She was glad, of course, to hear from him, but she had never asked herself why, precisely.

'...They are called typhoons...The mate did not seem to like it...Not in books...Couldn't think of letting it go on...'

The paper rustled sharply. '...A calm that lasted more than twenty minutes,' she read perfunctorily; and the next words her thoughtless eyes caught, on the top of another page, were: 'see you and the children again...' She had a movement of impatience. He was always thinking of coming home. He had never had such a good salary before. What was the matter now?

It did not occur to her to turn back overleaf to look. She would have found it recorded there that between 4 and 6 A. M. on December 25th, Captain MacWhirr did actually think that his ship could not possibly live another hour in such a sea, and that he would never see his wife and children again. Nobody was to know this (his letters got mislaid so quickly)—nobody whatever but the steward, who had been greatly impressed by that disclosure. So much so, that he tried to give the cook some idea of the 'narrow squeak we all had' by saying solemnly, 'The old man himself had a dam' poor opinion of our chance.'

'How do you know?' asked, contemptuously, the cook, an old soldier. 'He hasn't told you, maybe?'

'Well, he did give me a hint to that effect,' the steward brazened it out.

'Get along with you! He will be coming to tell me next,' jeered the old cook, over his shoulder.

Mrs MacWhirr glanced farther, on the alert. '...Do what's fair...Miserable objects.... Only three, with a broken leg each, and one...Thought had better keep the matter quiet...hope to have done the fair thing...'

She let fall her hands. No: there was nothing more about coming home. Must have been merely expressing a pious wish. Mrs MacWhirr's mind was set at ease, and a black marble clock, priced by the local jeweller at 3L. 18s. 6d., had a discreet stealthy tick.

The door flew open, and a girl in the long-legged, short-frocked period of existence, flung into the room.

A lot of colourless, rather lanky hair was scattered over her shoulders. Seeing her mother, she stood still, and directed her pale prying eyes upon the letter.

'From father,' murmured Mrs MacWhirr. 'What have you done with your ribbon?'

The girl put her hands up to her head and pouted.

'He's well,' continued Mrs MacWhirr languidly. 'At least I think so. He never says.' She had a little laugh. The girl's face expressed a wandering indifference, and Mrs MacWhirr surveyed her with fond pride.

'Go and get your hat,' she said after a while. 'I am going out to do some shopping. There is a sale at Linom's.'

'Oh, how jolly!' uttered the child, impressively, in unexpectedly grave vibrating tones, and bounded out of the room.

It was a fine afternoon, with a gray sky and dry sidewalks. Outside the draper's Mrs MacWhirr smiled upon a woman in a black mantle of generous proportions armoured in jet and crowned with flowers blooming falsely above a bilious matronly countenance. They broke into a swift little babble of greetings and exclamations both together, very hurried, as if the street were ready to yawn open and swallow all that pleasure before it could be expressed.

Behind them the high glass doors were kept on the swing. People couldn't pass, men stood aside waiting patiently, and Lydia was absorbed in poking the end of her parasol between the stone flags. Mrs MacWhirr talked rapidly.

'Thank you very much. He's not coming home yet. Of course it's very sad to have him away, but it's such a comfort to know he keeps so well.' Mrs MacWhirr drew breath. 'The climate there agrees with him,' she added, beamingly, as if poor MacWhirr had been away touring in China for the sake of his health.

Neither was the chief engineer coming home yet. Mr Rout knew too well the value of a good billet.

'Solomon says wonders will never cease,' cried Mrs Rout joyously at the old lady in her armchair by the fire. Mr Rout's mother moved slightly, her withered hands lying in black half-mittens on her lap.

The eyes of the engineer's wife fairly danced on the paper. 'That captain of the ship he is in—a rather simple man, you remember, mother?—has done something rather clever, Solomon says.'

'Yes, my dear,' said the old woman meekly, sitting with bowed silvery head, and that air of inward stillness characteristic of very old people who seem lost in watching the last flickers of life. 'I think I remember.'

Solomon Rout, Old Sol, Father Sol, the Chief, 'Rout,

good man'—Mr Rout, the condescending and paternal friend of youth, had been the baby of her many children—all dead by this time. And she remembered him best as a boy of ten—long before he went away to serve his apprenticeship in some great engineering works in the North. She had seen so little of him since, she had gone through so many years, that she had now to retrace her steps very far back to recognize him plainly in the mist of time. Sometimes it seemed that her daughter-in-law was talking of some strange man.

Mrs Rout junior was disappointed. 'H'm. H'm.' She turned the page. 'How provoking! He doesn't say what it is. Says I couldn't understand how much there was in it. Fancy! What could it be so very clever? What a wretched man not to tell us!'

She read on without further remark soberly, and at last sat looking into the fire. The chief wrote just a word or two of the typhoon; but something had moved him to express an increased longing for the companionship of the jolly woman. 'If it hadn't been that mother must be looked after, I would send you your passage-money to-day. You could set up a small house out here. I would have a chance to see you sometimes then. We are not growing younger…'

'He's well, mother,' sighed Mrs Rout, rousing herself.

'He always was a strong healthy boy,' said the old woman, placidly.

But Mr Jukes' account was really animated and very full. His friend in the Western Ocean trade imparted it freely to the other officers of his liner. 'A chap I know writes to me about an extraordinary affair that happened on board his ship in that typhoon—you know—that we read of in the papers two months ago. It's the funniest thing! Just see for yourself what he says. I'll show you his letter.'

There were phrases in it calculated to give the impression of light-hearted, indomitable resolution. Jukes had written them in good faith, for he felt thus when he wrote. He described with lurid effect the scenes in the 'tween-deck. '…It struck me in a flash that those confounded Chinamen couldn't tell we weren't a desperate kind of robbers. 'Tisn't good to part the Chinaman from his money if he is the stronger party. We need have been desperate indeed to go thieving in such weather, but what could these beggars know of us? So, without thinking of it twice, I got the hands away in a jiffy. Our work was done—that the old man had set his heart on. We cleared out without staying to inquire how they felt. I am convinced that if they had not been so unmercifully shaken, and afraid—each individual one of them—to stand up, we would have been torn to pieces. Oh! It was pretty complete, I can tell you; and you may run to and fro across the Pond to the end of time before you find yourself with such a job on your hands.'

After this he alluded professionally to the damage done to the ship, and went on thus:

'It was when the weather quieted down that the situation became confoundedly delicate. It wasn't made any better by us having been lately transferred to the Siamese flag; though the skipper can't see that it makes any difference—'as long as we are on board'—he says. There are feelings that this man simply hasn't got—and there's an end of it. You might just as well try to make a bedpost understand. But apart from this it is an infernally lonely state for a ship to be going about the China seas with no proper consuls, not even a gunboat of her own anywhere, nor a body to go to in case of some trouble.

'My notion was to keep these Johnnies under hatches for another fifteen hours or so; as we weren't much farther than that from Fu-chau. We would find there, most likely, some sort of a man-of-war, and once under her guns we were safe enough; for surely any skipper of a man-of-war—English, French or Dutch—would see white men through as far as row on board goes. We could get rid of them and their money afterwards by delivering them to their Mandarin or Taotai, or whatever they call these chaps in goggles you see being carried about in sedan-chairs through their stinking streets.

'The old man wouldn't see it somehow. He wanted to keep the matter quiet. He got that notion into his head, and a steam windlass couldn't drag it out of him. He wanted as little fuss made as possible, for the sake of the ship's name and for the sake of the owners—'for the sake of all concerned,' says he, looking at me very hard.

'It made me angry hot. Of course you couldn't keep a thing like that quiet; but the chests had been secured in the usual manner and were safe enough for any earthly gale, while this had been an altogether fiendish business I couldn't give you even an idea of.

'Meantime, I could hardly keep on my feet. None of us had a spell of any sort for nearly thirty hours, and there the old man sat rubbing his chin, rubbing the top of his head, and so bothered he didn't even think of pulling his long boots off.

'I hope, sir,' says I, 'you won't be letting them out on deck before we make ready for them in some shape or other.' Not, mind you, that I felt very sanguine about controlling these beggars if they meant to take charge. A trouble with a cargo of Chinamen is no child's play. I was dam' tired, too. 'I wish,' said I, 'you would let us throw the whole lot of these dollars down to them and leave them to fight it out amongst themselves, while we get a rest.'

'Now you talk wild, Jukes,' says he, looking up in his slow way that makes you ache all over, somehow. 'We must plan out something that would be fair to all parties.'

'I had no end of work on hand, as you may imagine, so I set the hands going, and then I thought I would turn in a bit. I hadn't been asleep in my bunk ten minutes when in rushes the steward and begins to pull at my leg.

'For God's sake, Mr Jukes, come out! Come on deck quick, sir. Oh, do come out!'

'The fellow scared all the sense out of me. I didn't know what had happened: another hurricane—or what. Could hear no wind.

'The Captain's letting them out. Oh, he is letting them out! Jump on deck, sir, and save us. The chief engineer has just run below for his revolver.'

'That's what I understood the fool to say. However, Father Rout swears he went in there only to get a clean pocket-handkerchief. Anyhow, I made one jump into my trousers and flew on deck aft. There was certainly a good deal of noise going on forward of the bridge. Four of the hands with the boss'n were at work abaft. I passed up to them some of the rifles all the ships on the China coast carry in the cabin, and led them on the bridge. On the way I ran against Old Sol, looking startled and sucking at an unlighted cigar.

'Come along,' I shouted to him.

'We charged, the seven of us, up to the chart-room. All was over. There stood the old man with his sea-boots still drawn up to the hips and in shirt-sleeves—got warm thinking it out, I suppose. Bun Hin's dandy clerk at his elbow, as dirty as a sweep, was still green in the face. I could see directly I was in for something.

'What the devil are these monkey tricks, Mr Jukes?' asks the old man, as angry as ever he could be. I tell you frankly it made me lose my tongue. 'For God's sake, Mr Jukes,' says he, 'do take away these rifles from the men. Somebody's sure to get hurt before long if you don't. Damme, if this ship isn't worse than Bedlam! Look sharp now. I want you up here to help me and Bun Hin's Chinaman to count that money. You wouldn't mind lending a hand, too, Mr Rout, now you are here. The more of us the better.'

'He had settled it all in his mind while I was having a snooze. Had we been an English ship, or only going to land our cargo of coolies in an English port, like Hong-Kong, for instance, there would have been no end of inquiries and bother, claims for damages and so on. But these Chinamen know their officials better than we do.

'The hatches had been taken off already, and they were all on deck after a night and a day down below. It made you feel queer to see so many gaunt, wild faces together. The beggars stared about at the sky, at the sea, at the ship, as though they had expected the whole thing to have been blown to pieces. And no wonder! They had had a doing that would have shaken the soul out of a white man. But then they say a Chinaman has no soul. He has, though, something about him that is deuced tough. There was a fellow (amongst others of the badly hurt) who had had his eye all but knocked out. It stood out of his head the size of half a hen's egg. This would have laid out a white man on his back for a month: and yet there was that chap elbowing here and there in the crowd and talking to the others as if nothing had been the matter. They made a great hubbub amongst themselves, and whenever the old man showed his bald head on the foreside of the bridge, they would all leave off jawing and look at him from below.

'It seems that after he had done his thinking he made that Bun Hin's fellow go down and explain to them the only way they could get their money back. He told me afterwards that, all the coolies having worked in the same place and for the same length of time, he reckoned he would be doing the fair thing by them as near as possible if he shared all the cash we had picked up equally among the lot. You couldn't tell one man's dollars from another's, he said, and if you asked each man how much money he brought on board he was afraid they would lie, and he would find himself a long way short. I think he was right there. As to giving up the money to any Chinese official he could scare up in Fu-chau, he said he might just as well put the lot in his own pocket at once for all the good it would be to them. I suppose they thought so, too.

'We finished the distribution before dark. It was rather a sight: the sea running high, the ship a wreck to look at, these Chinamen staggering up on the bridge one by one for their share, and the old man still booted, and in his shirt-sleeves, busy paying out at the chartroom door, perspiring like anything, and now and then coming down sharp on myself or Father Rout about one thing or another not quite to his mind. He took the share of those who were disabled himself to them on the No. 2 hatch. There were three dollars left over, and these went to the three most damaged coolies, one to each. We turned-to afterwards, and shovelled out on deck heaps of wet rags, all sorts of fragments of things without shape, and that you couldn't give a name to, and let them settle the ownership themselves.

'This certainly is coming as near as can be to keeping the thing quiet for the benefit of all concerned. What's your opinion, you pampered mail-boat swell? The old chief says that this was plainly the only thing that could be done. The skipper remarked to me the other day, 'There are things you find nothing about in books.' I think that he got out of it very well for such a stupid man.'